Dance of the

Ariadnes

Dance of the Ariadnes

Sharon Spencer

Spencer, Sharon.
    Dance of the Ariadnes/Sharon Spencer.
    ISBN 0-9652364-2-0
    LCCN 98-60975

Dedicated to Srdjan

who was there

Acknowledgements:

Special thanks to Dolores Brandon, Diana Balsama, Ann Liddell, Lynn Sands Herron, and Erika Herron for their assistance.

Preface

Among the many friends of my late sister Anaïs Nin, Sharon Spencer is unique. She understood Anaïs's continuing struggle arising from her "four-chambered heart." Close to Anaïs, her husband Hugo, and Rupert Pole, Sharon spared no effort to embrace them all with her openness and warmth.

One of the sources of inspiration for Sharon may have been *The Novel of the Future*, which provides more of a guide to what to avoid than where to go.

Anaïs nurtured that thought, affected as she was by other influences all of her literary life, never quite losing the independence of the self-taught or the desire to explore the hidden or the unknown. Too often, it appeared that she was encumbered by her success and forced to take a stand she had not contemplated.

Sharon Spencer was one of the exceptions. She admired Anaïs for what she was and loved her for what she did while accepting everything she gave. No two people could have had more different backgrounds, particularly in the area of literature. Sharon disciplined from the start, Anaïs undisciplined to the end.

And yet they were profoundly respectful of each other's strengths and weaknesses, with Anaïs never wanting Sharon to change.

And now Anaïs cannot read Sharon's new book and Sharon will not have the satisfaction of knowing how pleased she would have been with it. Of that I am certain. For Sharon has the one trait that Anaïs admired above all others: the ability, the courage, and the inner wisdom of being herself.

Joaquín Nin-Culmell
Oakland, California 1998

Introduction

If *The Novel of the Future* is an example of Anaïs Nin's influence on me, then an example of our affinity is *The Seduction of the Minotaur*, a brilliant work that follows Lillian, the lead character, on her excruciating but at times enjoyable path through her personal psychic labyrinth. *Seduction* and *Dance of the Ariadnes* both explore events emanating from the Palace of Knossos in Minoan Crete, but in quite different ways.

My intent (albeit unconscious until I had seen what I was writing) was to reanimate a myth that is both illuminating and terrifying. In fact, neither of my book's "Ariadnes" (Miranda and Divna) is profoundly given to introspection, as is Lillian. Both are artists, the one a painter, the other an actress who usually performs ancient Greek tragedies. Both Miranda and Divna are "real" and at the same time mythic. They are re-imaginings of the ancient vegetation goddess Ariadne, whose name in Greek ("Ari Hagne") means "the most holy."

The mythic and historic Ariadne was the most sacred figure in the civilization of Minoan Crete. She was priestess, goddess and a real woman, who, one version of the story tells us, was briefly disloyal to her consort Dionysios. She fell in love with the mainland Greek conqueror Theseus, whom she armed with a sword and also aided in finding his way out of the treacherous labyrinth. This maze, or labyrinth (one of five mentioned by ancient writers) was allegedly constructed for Ariadne's father King Minos as a prison for her half-brother, the Minotaur. After Theseus killed the Minotaur, he and Ariadne escaped from Crete altogether. When they reached the island of Dia (Naxos), Theseus repaid Ariadne's passionate generosity by abandoning her. (This is only one version of a story that has several endings.) Ariadne was rescued by Dionysios and became his bride. Of Ariadne, the renowned scholar Walter F. Otto wrote: "She is the queen of the Dionysiac women. She alone is worthy to stand at the side of Dionysios and to become the only one who is raised by him into immortality."

Dionysios (Bacchus, in Roman adaptation) is the god of wine and poetic inspiration. He is the god "who comes," a "stranger" god, probably from Asia Minor, and his followers are primarily women, who are known as Maenads. His primary instinctual associations are to lions and panthers. He is powerful but very dangerous, as such men are to gullible women. He is a figure of human suffering but to other people he brings inspiration and regeneration. On the human level, he is simply a very attractive and seductive male (suggested by an actual Greek singer-songwriter).

However, neither Miranda nor Divna needs the inspiration of a man to ignite their creativity. Both are self-generated, self-motivated, self-actualizing artists. But they are also women who love and who want to be loved. They are willing to suffer and they are more than capable of withstanding life's frustrations and sorrows. Again, to quote Walter F. Otto: "Ariadne is a mortal Aphrodite. It belongs to the nature of the Dionysiac that life and death, mortality and eternity are mixed up with one another in a miraculous way in those who are near to the god.... The women with whom he is most intimately associated reach a state of glory only by passing through deep sorrow." And so it is with Miranda and Divna, both of whom are privileged, or cursed, to live forever with their enigmatic and alluring lover/husband, Dionysios.

Dance of the Ariadnes is an invitation to enter this ancient tale through the lives of my characters, the artists Miranda, Divna and Dionysios.

Sharon Spencer
Upper Montclair, New Jersey 1998

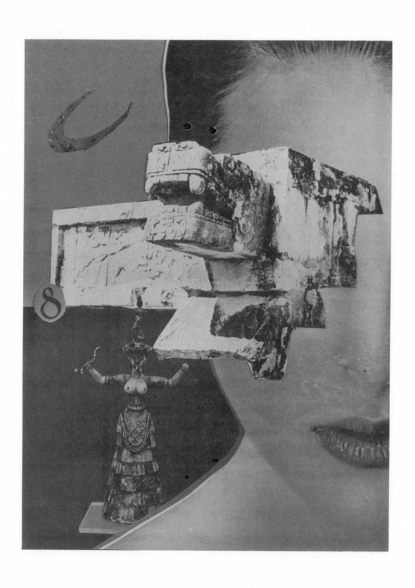

The goddess falls in love with Herself, drawing forth her own emanation, which takes on a life of its own. Love of self for self is the creative force of the universe. Desire is the primal energy; and that energy is erotic.

(Starhawk, The Spiral Dance)

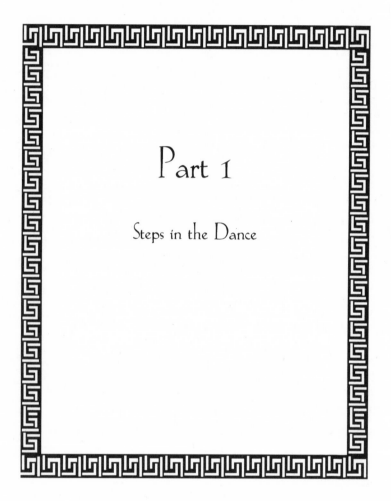

Part 1

Steps in the Dance

Yadwigha, peacefully asleep,
enjoys a lovely dream:
she hears a kind snake charmer
playing upon his reed.
On stream and foliage glisten
the silvery beams of the moon;
and savage serpents listen
to the gay entrancing tune.

(Henri "Douanier" Rousseau)

Closing her book, Miranda turns out the light. For a while she rests against the pillow, sipping retsina, warm but still tasting like pine woods, pleasantly medicinal on the tongue. She sometimes drinks wine before she goes to sleep; sometimes when her brain is drugged, images arise from the depths of her subterranean mind, floating upward to splinter the surface of consciousness with a shattering impact, images propelled toward explosion by the pressure with which they have been locked into the icehouse of memory. At such times the force of the charge is so brutal that it shakes her out of her reverie, sending her to work on a painting.

But not now. She is burdened by a "block," and she has also suffered a more classical affliction—she has recently been abandoned by a man she cared for deeply.

Savoring a sip of retsina, she swallows it slowly, reluctantly, allowing the sensation of the warm wine to conjure a vision of a forest washed with shafts of yellow light, saturated with melody by the songs of unseen birds, cooled by winds that create a music of their own as they play the branches of the trees like slender fingers coaxing chords from the strings of a lyre. Allowing herself to sink deeper into the music of the night, she fervently embraces visions of paintings she hasn't yet begun.

In the hot night on the island of Crete, Miranda imagines herself inside the Palace of Knossos where she strolls among the frescoes, admiring the slender deep-waisted young men whose black curls hang to their shoulders, young men whose elegant headdresses sweep back from their brows, enhancing their firmly drawn profiles with the arching curve of a crown worn rakishly above the brow. Each forehead is adorned by three flat black curls. Young men dressed in magnificent gold breast plates and loincloths layered over their taut thighs, images of flawless manliness. Princes of the Lilies, colored in peacock blue and a dull gold, colors that seem to signify an era of perfectly equilibrated harmony.

The men! Ever since *the* man went away without an explanation, Miranda hasn't painted anything new. Worse, she has been obsessed with sensual dreams to which she abandons herself again and again with the relentless submission of a sleepwalker. She dreams but cannot understand the meaning of her dreams.

She is bent low, crouching above a prone figure, her knees pressed into the earth on either side of a body that lies motionless between her spread legs. Arching back for a moment, she lunges forward, ploughing the air with a sweeping motion as sinuous as the smoothly arched throat of a swan about to snatch its prey from under the surface of a still, sunny pond. Gradually, she lowers her open thighs around a penis as hard as stone, and, crouching, she grinds her body slightly from side to side to work the penis to the full length of its shaft. Raising her buttocks in the air, she rocks and sways until she can feel the tip of the penis striking the entrance to her womb, striking, grazing repeatedly like a match igniting a circle of quiescent flame. Hips and buttocks clenched, tightly grasping the penis, she slowly, languorously begins moving forward and backward in long gliding motions that rub the penis in and out. She quickens her rhythm, muscles tightening around the penis which seems to flow in liquid sweetness. She presses her knees against the statue's motionless flanks as she rides him backward and forward, up and down the corridor of her body.

A panic. Her nerves begin to vibrate to the rotation of her glistening center upon the hard stone of the lingam. Nerves send tiny whiplashes of sensation streaking through her belly. Inside her body, a fluttering as though hundreds of birds take flight all at once, soaring in soft implosion, firing every organ, nerve and muscle to incendiary orgasm.

Perspiring, exhausted, finally she flings herself backward, head and throat arched, her hands clutching the warm earth. Still astride the statue, she stares, as if surprised, at the liquid flowing down the insides of her thighs, stares at her knees planted deep in the grainy black earth where moist leaves and flowers lie scattered.

Miranda wakes up. She lies in the dark, heart beating quickly. She feels frightened and oddly hungry, even though she has eaten very satisfyingly earlier at the Dolphin Café. In her room there is nothing to eat. Only half a bottle of retsina. Pulling herself from the nest of damp sheets, she pours a cup of wine and sits clutching it in both hands, propped against the wall with her knees raised in a simple posture that had always reassured her when she was a child, terrified by a nightmare whose gargantuan comicstrip threats refused to be absorbed by the depths of innocent sleep. Supported by a heap of soft pillows, she gradually realizes, even though the realization is dulled by the soothing taste of the retsina, that in her dream the statue she had straddled was, in fact, not a man at all but the avatar, Osiris, she has restored to life.

Willing herself to the numbness that precedes sleep, she gradually becomes aware of the night music.

Outside her window is an air shaft that rises the height of the hotel, a vertical tunnel where sounds emerge from the windows of the guests' rooms, meet, collide, become magnified, and produce a composition sufficiently harsh to be torture to her ears. The whimpering of a puppy. A squalling baby. Low, excited, amorous voices. And a final ironic note, surprisingly intrusive, of the Brahms Symphony Number Three, a ponderous construct of sounds that assault the night air. Here on the island of Crete in the sweetly scented summer night, laden with the perfume of basil, someone is playing, repeatedly playing, a tape of Brahms' Symphony Number Three.

Eventually, however, she falls asleep, stunned by the blend of warm wine nursed from a paper cup and the overbearing music of a culture from which she has run away, for when she left the United States for that other island where she lived and painted for a time, she felt as joyous as a kite soaring toward heaven, its mooring severed by a reckless but confident hand.

Both hands grasping string bags stuffed with peppers, potatoes, corn, bread, and several bottles of wine, plus cans and cartons, I pushed my way through the passengers and got off the packed bus. I would walk the rest of the way. Sweat was pouring down my face and neck, making my skin prickle. My thin blouse was soaked....

It was just 2:00. As usual, I was a little late, tired and frustrated too. I'd wasted the entire morning going from one government bureau to another. And I hadn't gotten what I needed, after all! Four small pieces of paper! That was all! But they had to be cut free from governmental red tape.

I unlocked the door of the large gray building, welcoming its interior coolness. The narrow halls were filled with the smells of garlic and oil, of cabbage and onions frying. The halls always smelled this way. Anyhow, Aunt Mileva would have a good meal waiting. That was some comfort, at least.

Mileva opened the door and stood waiting with her arms open. "Divna, my dear, you look worn out!"

"I am!" I dropped the bags and hugged her. "Guess what? I didn't get the visas."

"Of course not." Mileva shook her head. She was covered by a red and blue checked apron. When she smiled, her gold teeth shone. Her two upper teeth were widely spaced, and she had two round red spots on her cheeks from spending so much time at the stove, I thought.

Grinning, she said, "Well, that's what you get for marrying a Greek instead of someone from your own country."

"But I don't even live with him any more," I wailed, feeling enormous relief at being able to complain to someone who wouldn't mind listening. My arms ached from carrying those heavy bags so far. I peeled off my blouse and skirt, kicked off my high heels and carried the food back to the small kitchen in the rear of the apartment.

"You'll get the visas tomorrow," Mileva announced with assurance. "I've been reading the cards. They're never wrong. The Greek government wants you to perform for their people. How can our stupid officials refuse to give you the permits? They just want to make you wait—punish you a little bit for marrying that stupid Greek."

Sighing with relief—because I was free, at least for a while, from the morning's frustrations—I fanned my sweaty face. Throwing back my head, I let fly a string of curses.

Aunt Mileva was probably right about why the officials at the immigration service were being so stubborn. I sat down at the table in my slip and stockinged feet. "Did Sasha stop sneezing this morning?"

"Yes, his nose improved. And so did your daughter's disposition. What a princess! She has her father's arrogance!"

Aunt Mileva brought me a large bowl of chicken soup with a piece of rye bread and a poached egg floating in it.

"You're right. She has her father's sense of self-importance. I wish she had his good looks too!"

Mileva chuckled, moving around the little kitchen, placing knives and forks and napkins on the table. Next, several hunks of brown bread, a dish of roasted peppers seasoned with olive oil and garlic, and, finally, a salad of tomatoes, peppers and parsley. After this we drank several cups of Turkish coffee.

"Still haven't gotten over him, have you, my girl?" Aunt Mileva turned back to the stove and stirred a pot. "Oh, I almost forgot to tell you. Tony Tomato called."

"That ass!"

Mileva sat down and handed me a glass of slivovitz. We raised our glasses, clinked them together and rapidly toasted each other. "He's only an ass when you compare him to the *other* one!" She rolled her eyes.

"Bruno's an ass," I muttered. "But he's all there is right now."

This was our dinner, eaten early in the afternoon. In the evenings I'd have a piece of cheese and a salad. But by two in the afternoon I was always hungry, having been up since five, washing and dressing the children for school, dressing myself and taking a bus across the city to the State Theater.

"Tsk! Tsk!" Mileva playfully scolded as she set a steaming platter down between us. It was heaped with chunks of boiled beef surrounded by carrots and potatoes. Beside the platter, a bowl of horseradish.

Sitting down again, Mileva shook her head in wonder. "Divna, my girl, for a pretty woman you've known some men with feathers in their heads."

"Feathers, you say! Not Dionysios! His head's stuffed with rocks!"

"Marry a man named Dionysios," she muttered. "Any fool could see what would come of that!"

"Close your mouth so no more words will come out," I said, with a friendly laugh.

Mileva patted my shoulder. "Don't worry about the re-entry permits. You'll even get one for Tony Tomato."

At least "Tony Tomato" wasn't as insulting as "pig's ass," which was what Mileva usually called Dionysios, at least after we got separated. Legally, we were still married.

"Well, then, how are the rehearsals going?"

"Okay," I lied. Actually, the man—the boy—playing opposite me in "Hippolytus" was a serious problem. But I didn't want to waste energy talking about him now. I would have to work with him for the rest of the day. And I was tired.

I lay down on the couch, closing my eyes. Mileva kept the shades down in summer, so the apartment was cool. The dim light also veiled the shabbiness of the furniture and the rugs. My thoughts drifted to the role of Phaedra. A woman totally possessed by erotic attraction. Phaedra. It was very challenging, and I loved the difficulty.

After the rehearsal I had to pick up the laundry, meet Tamara and Sasha at their school, buy a few more vegetables and some white cheese, and try to make myself look as decent as possible to go out dancing with Bruno. Aunt Mileva was right. He wasn't very smart and he wasn't very good with my children. But I still wanted him to go to Greece with us. I was much too proud to go to the country of my husband's birth without a male companion. It was just pride—stupid pride, maybe. For that matter, with a lot less pride on both sides, who knows whether Dionysios and I might have still been together.

I knew I should break up with Bruno and every day I promised myself I'd do it. I'd do it, I told myself again, as soon as we got back from Greece.

Meanwhile, I opened one eye and glanced at the clock. Ten more minutes before I had to put my clothes back on and go into the hot crowded streets, fight crowds to get on the bus, and fight them again to get off the bus. The second round-trip in one day!

I tried to remember the name of the government official who

admired me and always sent flowers before my openings. I hoped maybe he could help me untangle some of the red tape keeping me from getting the permits. But I couldn't think of the guy's name! Maybe Dushko, my director, would remember it.

While I dozed Mileva sat in an armchair fanning herself with a magazine. The whishing sounds helped me rest.

After a while she gently shook my shoulder. I'd fallen asleep. I was snoring. I groaned, heaved my legs off the couch and stood up.

People think actresses have such glamorous lives!

It was nearly four. People were going back to work after their dinner breaks. At seven they'd be free again for a few hours. Everyone seemed cranky, as if they'd taken naps and awakened in rotten moods. They jostled one another with undisguised aggression. A few grumbled curses and even shook their fists. A guy shoved his prick against my thigh and rubbed. "Watch it!" I yelled. I almost slapped his face. Surprised, he stared at me, then grinned and opened his mouth as if to say something I was pretty sure I didn't want to hear.

It was a relief to get to the cool dark theater, and when I ducked inside, I felt calmer right away, even less worried about the visas. For the first time it occurred to me that the director of the theater should really take charge of getting the visas. After all, I was the mainstay of the national company. Why hadn't I thought of this before? It was just my way to accept responsibility automatically for almost anything that had to be done. What an ass I was!

I sat down and kicked off my tight shoes. Like all my clothes, my shoes were cheap and didn't fit well. I was paid decently for my work, but besides partially supporting the children, I also supported Aunt Mileva. There was nothing left for luxuries, like good shoes.

The theater smelled of soap and clean rags and mops. I loved it! So much fresher than the baking streets and sweating people. I began to think about Phaedra. Passionate, single-minded, even obsessed. Yes, and obsessive too, while I was practical, rooted, always taking care of the things I thought had to be done. But Phaedra was totally ruled by her emotions. She sacrificed everything—reputation, marriage, honor, even her life for an unattainable love! All fire, Phaedra! And I, an earthling, stuck in the mud. Was this why I found it so hard to break up with Bruno, because in a very basic way he fulfilled me? I sat musing over these thoughts, but especially over my grand idea, more like a vision, of the way I wanted to portray Phaedra. It was almost like praying, sitting in the dark theater dreaming of ways to express a woman who was so different from myself.

"Divna! Divna!" Dushko had to whisper my name several times before he succeeded in breaking into my reverie. He was my director, my co-worker and also my friend. He sat down in the next seat. We kissed each other on both cheeks and sat holding hands for a few minutes.

"You were lost in your thoughts," he commented, giving my hand a little squeeze.

"Dreaming of Phaedra. I just love this role!"

He smiled with a touch of pride. "That's obvious. You'll grow from it, Divna. You're learning a lot. But what are we going to do about the cowboy?"

I shook my head. "The problem is, he has no talent. And he's spoiled and arrogant. If he lacked talent but had a good attitude, then maybe...."

Dushko was shaking his head almost violently. "I'm going to

get rid of him. I have a plan."

I was incredulous. "How can you get rid of him! We both know his father runs the army!"

Dushko rolled his eyes and gave me a smirk. "Never mind. I have good connections at Cinecittá. I'm going to arrange for the cowboy to have a film audition in Rome. You'll see how long he hangs around a national theater that does classical plays!"

"Sounds good!" I pressed Dushko's arm. He was clever. A person had to be to remain in charge of any government enterprise for more than a month. "Isn't it peaceful here, Dushko?" I gazed around the theater again.

"It's your church, Divna."

I nodded. Then I said quickly, "Listen, there are several things I don't like about my interpretation. I thought I might get some ideas from looking at Martha Graham's notes for her dance about Phaedra. What do you think?"

Dushko turned his pale gray eyes on me, and they were filled with an admiration that was the most satisfying experience of the day so far. His admiration was warmed by real love; he was made happy, really happy, by my ambition to do this work as well as I possibly could. "A very good idea, love. 'Voices of Desire' it was called."

I stood up and wriggled my puffy feet back into my stupid high-heeled shoes.

Watching my struggle, Dushko exclaimed, "I've never been able to believe that a woman as sensible as you would wear those things. Why?"

"Because I'm an ass," I replied cheerfully. "You know it's my vanity. I just want to look as tall as I can."

Dushko laughed, shaking his head. "You're practically an Amazon in your bare feet!" He patted my rump tenderly.

"A gentle Amazon, Dushko."

I had caught sight of my co-star; he was posed at the doorway, waiting for Dushko and me to notice him. Even though it was nearly a hundred degrees outside, he was wearing a black leather jacket upholstered in studs. Skin-tight jeans that outlined his genitals and an Italian-style shirt open to his navel. He was grinning, deepening the two clefts in his tanned cheeks.

"Hi, Giorgio!" Dushko called out with a faint note of mockery that the cowboy wasn't smart enough to catch. "Divna and I've been talking about how to improve your interpretation of Hippolytus. Do you have any new ideas?"

Giorgio thrust out his chin and clamped his hands on his pelvic bones.

"Excuse me, Dushko. I think I'll go back and put on my rehearsal smock."

When I reached the door to my dressing room, Dushko called, "Oh Divna, Tony Tomato called."

I groaned. I should never have told Dushko that Aunt Mileva called Bruno that stupid name. Now the entire company knew that my lover was a family joke!

I greeted the other women and took off my skirt and blouse. They were both rumpled, dirty and not very fresh-smelling. As I was slipping into a comfortable old rag, one of the actresses asked:

"What are we going to do about the punk?"

"He's going to ruin the production," another said. "He hasn't even read the play. Or else he's too stupid to understand it. Do you know, he's complaining that you're too old to play opposite him." Everyone giggled.

I turned and stared at the woman who'd said this. "'Too old!'

Obviously, he doesn't know what the play's about."

"Lepsha, you know he can't read. The only head he has is the one between his legs. You must have noticed that."

"He certainly *wants* us to notice it," said another, snickering. "How do you like his motorcycle get-up? He just saw 'Rebel Without a Cause' on television last week."

We all laughed. But it wasn't funny. I sat down and clutched my head in my hands, swaying from side to side. I wanted to laugh. I wanted to cry. Both at the same time. There was nothing we could do but trust that Dushko could manage to lure the cowboy off to Rome with the offer of a screen test.

Meanwhile, I had to go to Greece for a tour. After that, a vacation. I still didn't have any visas for the children, myself or Tony Tom—Bruno, that is. I had to phone him too. All my clothes were dirty and most of them needed mending. I had to get my hair cut before I went to Greece. My son had either a chronic cold or an allergy. And my daughter couldn't think about anything except her great love for her marvelous father, the great Greek folk singer. I still hadn't done a thing to get a divorce. If I were divorced from Dionysios I probably wouldn't be having such problems crossing the Greek border. Why didn't I, who was usually so quick to see the practical side of anything, just get a divorce?

The door opened and Dushko stuck his head inside the dressing room. "Divna, there's something I forgot to tell you."

Sighing, I answered: "I know. The cowboy thinks I'm too old to do love scenes with him. I know he's only seventeen, but doesn't he know I'm portraying his stepmother?"

"Don't worry about that. He's learning the story right now. No, it isn't that. A messenger has just come from the Immigration Office. He has the re-entry permits."

I jumped up and hugged him. "What a good friend you are! My heart is lighter by pounds!"

"You go to Greece. It'll do you good. After that, take a vacation. When you come back to finish rehearsals, you'll have a new co-star. I promise."

That night when I was putting the children to bed, Tamara lifted her frowning face and asked: "Mamma, why don't you and my father live together?" I was about to kiss her but I waited and she added the complaint that other kids' mothers and fathers lived together.

"You know your father is a Greek and he lives in Greece. At least, sometimes." This didn't seem to be a convincing reason, so I stroked her cheek and explained: "I'm sorry we don't live together any longer. I know you'd like that better, but sometimes grownups have to make decisions that—"

Sasha sneezed loudly. Then again, and again and again. He sneezed violently eight times in quick succession.

Screwing her face into a grimace, Tamara turned to the wall. "He always does that when I'm trying to talk to you!" She sniffed. "He's such a damned baby! Why don't you ever notice that Sasha always sneezes when I'm trying to talk to you?" She pressed her eyes closed but tears seeped under the lids.

In the act of handing Sasha a tissue, I paused to wonder. Maybe Tamara was right. I'd never thought about the possibility that Sasha's chronic sneezing was a way of attracting attention to himself. I'd been too busy to notice. Too busy with my work, too busy with Bruno.

"Darling, do you feel all right?" I murmured, wiping Sasha's nose. I put my palm on his forehead but his temperature seemed normal. Sasha cried a little, gathered his strength and blew his nose hard in the tissue I held in my hand. I felt the mucus spurt against my skin, tearing the tissue.

"Stay home, Mamma," Sasha begged. He grabbed my hand and kissed it. At my back Tamara lay snuffling into her pillow; her face was turned to the wall.

Suddenly, she sat up in bed, whining, "Are you going to marry Tony Tomato?"

Sasha started giggling. Obviously, he wasn't very sick.

"No, and don't call him that, Tamara."

"Do I have to go to Greece with you?" Sasha muttered, snuffling. "I don't want to go. I want to stay here with Aunt Mileva."

I stood up. "You're both acting like babies. I've spent the whole day doing things for all of us. And now I'm going out for a few hours. Yes, we're all going to Greece. No, I'm not going to marry Bruno. Legally, your father and I are still married."

Tamara seemed more cheerful when she heard this. Rolling away from the wall, she turned on her back and opened her eyes. "Sasha, you're stupid. Don't you want to go to Greece to see your father?"

Sasha sneezed, then said, "I don't know if I do or I don't."

"Good night," I said. I closed the door behind me.

As usual, I had nothing nice to wear. Bruno always looked like he'd been modeling clothes in a shop off the Piazza DiSpagna in Rome. Digging around in my closet, I came up with a red dress that had only been worn once or twice but had a torn belt. I reached into a battered shoebox where I kept scarves and found one that vaguely matched the dress. Twisting it tightly, I belted the dress. I'd never cared much about clothes. It was just as well because I'd never been able to afford more than a few cheap dresses. Dionysios hadn't cared at all. He had jokingly suggested that I wear a draped sheet. But Bruno was different. I think the scrappy way I got myself together embarrassed him.

I tied a scarf over my hair, hurried through the living room where Aunt Mileva was sitting, nodding half asleep as she watched the news on television. A ball of black yarn had fallen out of her chair and rolled across the rug.

"Enjoy yourself, Lepsha," she said in a sweet voice, adding, "But try not to stay out too late. You have such a hard schedule."

Bruno was waiting at the curb, motorcycle idling. Long legs astride his bike, he was smoking and working one of the pedals up and down. I got on behind him and wrapped my arms around his trim waist. He revved up the cycle and we shot off down the street. We were going to our favorite place, a little club where there was American music and cheap wine.

I pressed my breasts against Bruno's back. It was exhilarating to be so close to his body. I loved the way he smelled. It had taken a while, but finally I had persuaded Bruno to give up using scented deodorants (he thought they were smart, sophisticated, American).

I loved the speed of the cycle. I loved roaring up and down the streets of Beograd, weaving in and out around the fast-moving cars. I loved turning corners sharply, the bike tilting, then righting itself. It was dangerous. It was exciting. The swift movement seemed to wipe out all the problems of the day. It refreshed me.

When we arrived at the street where the club was located, Bruno made a sharp turn. The brakes squealed. I jumped off the bike with an elastic bounce.

Cocking his head, Bruno looked me up and down and winked. "You look swell," he said, using a word that always made us giggle. It was so American, so out-of-date, so comical sounding.

"You too. You look swell," I returned, happily. I threw my arms around Bruno and we kissed, a long kiss hinting at the pleasure we would give each other later after we had drunk wine and danced.

Inside, it was dark and smoky. The waiter knew us well and so did the "D.J.," who waved as she shuffled through a stack of records.

As soon as we were sitting down and our wine was served, Bruno handed me a small package wrapped in purple paper. "This is to wish you good luck in Greece."

He looked very handsome. His brown hair was thick and shiny, and his eyes were a soft shade of green that he usually accentuated by wearing blue or green shirts. "After this tour you'll be too famous to go around with an ordinary guy like me."

"Oh no I won't!" I felt guilty because I was planning to break up with him. Why should I, after all, if I enjoyed being with him? It was nobody else's business, was it?

I unwrapped Bruno's gift. It was perfume, "Anaïs, Anaïs." The gift was his way of drawing a parallel between the writer and myself. At times he could be very sweet, and I felt ashamed of letting people call him "Tony Tomato."

We danced for a couple of hours. Our favorite music was very dated, classic rock and roll and rhythm and blues. We even tried to dance to jazz. We looked good together, Bruno and I. We were about the same height and had the same intense, almost violent way of moving as our bodies spelled out the vibrant, sometimes angry rhythms of the music we loved.

Later, after we'd gone to Bruno's apartment, we undressed each other with impatient hands and fell on his bed. With almost no preliminary caresses, we pushed close together and Bruno entered me. We rolled from side to side, mouths pressed together, hands clutching each other. We had hardly finished when we began over again.

Just before we said good night at about two in the morning, I remembered to tell Bruno I had gotten—that is, that Dushko had gotten the paperwork we needed to re-enter Yugoslavia from Greece. We were finally ready, everything was now ready for us to go to Greece.

I will meet him early in the morning at the entrance to the excavation site. His eyes will be mossy green, filled with glittering points of gold like a cat's, lighting the dark on a moonless night. He will be lean and blond, dirty dark blond like a street cat whose tough little triangular face burns with greedy terror. Furtive, the sleek movements of his small head and his long muscular legs. When he wants to escape he can run quickly. I can easily imagine his blond furriness stretched out in the sun. He will seem deceptively soft because of the golden down growing on his hands and forearms. And when he opens his mouth, he will reveal two rows of sharp white teeth. I can hear him, scratching and howling as he slinks through the streets at night, hugging the walls of the buildings, turning his back to people who might be passing by just when he unzips his pants, slips one deft downy hand inside to remove his penis. He will cradle it in his palm for a moment before relieving himself against a wall.

Green-eyed and golden, his furry little mouth open, the stranger will be wearing faded jeans and a soft black shirt when he approaches me in the morning at the excavation site, beckoning with an insolent smile.

I, who have never before followed a stranger anywhere, will yield under the caress of the manic sun, lighting me inside, like a lamp made from a large conch with a tiny red bulb planted deep inside its inner cavern, like the lamp that made my childhood room glow with a circle of caressing light, subduing the fears that invaded me as soon as the door closed on my mother's back.

In the morning there will be the rhythmic clicking of the cicadas. The warm ivory stones. The chunks of marble lying all over the ground, emanating rays of buttery sunlight, pulsating rays of light that will warm the dew that glitters on the grass. The stones will radiate heat to the same vibrations as the rhythm kept by the cicadas, the summer percussion, the insistent rhythm of August on the island of Crete, a music that strikes, that holds the perfect chord for the time, for the place, for the hunger, this hunger that cannot be appeased, has not been appeased since he left me on the island I can no longer claim as home.

Neither goddess nor queen, I will submit and he will lead; he will lead me through avenues of cypresses raising their foliage like huge feathery dark green arms welcoming us into the depths of a thick wood, a sprawl of moss across the low-lying valley behind the labyrinth. He will turn, then glance at me for a second, flashing me a look of laughing anticipation. And I will return his glance of taunting desire, feeling sly and feral as I trail after him into the gaping dark mouth of the woods.

Lost for a time in the shadows, we will run and play, cavorting and frolicking, teasing, brushing against each other's bodies, mine large and soft, his hard and purposeful, bristling with golden fur. My hair will fly wildly, tumbling around my shoulders and down my back, heavy hair, wetting my skin with hints of royal funk.

Deep in the depths of the shade in the wood behind the labyrinth, we will circle each other, breathing so heavily we can hear each other circling, pacing the earth, eyes locked in the obsessive stare of our mating dance. Gazes interpenetrating, lips glistening, perspiring heavily, we will trace circular patterns through the woods as we wheel and turn, retreating, advancing, first one, then the other, then one, then the other. Our conspiratorial ardor emits the odor of damp leaves disintegrating in a warm spring rain.

I will stop suddenly and stand with my back against the rough bark of a tall tree and I will pose for several seconds before arching back my head and neck. Lowering my eyes, I will stare at him, waiting, perspiring in my dark purple dress, drenched by the weight of my tangled black curls. He will stand in front of me, crouching slightly, his green-gold eyes focused on my nipples, hard little circles poking the fabric of my dress. Slowly, I will raise my skirt and hold it above my thighs near the bushy growth of black curls.

He will watch. He will not move as I insert a forefinger under my pretense of panties, a pink bikini. He will not move but only watch as I slowly pull the panties down, bend over and step out of them very slowly, leaving a puff of pink on the dark leaf-littered dirt.

Eyes lowered still, I will lean back against the tree, holding my skirt above my waist with one hand while with the other I will stroke the rosy gleam between my thighs.

The stranger will watch.

My turn to watch. He will languidly undo his pants as he walks closer without interrupting or diminishing the intensity of his gaze. Fingers flicking inside my body, burning like tiny flames, I will moan softly, inviting him to come closer. Abruptly, I will change my movements. With the palm of my hand I will cup the wet pink lips, molding a circle of entry. And with one long slow twisting motion he will penetrate me, impaling me against the tree trunk.

For long seconds our bodies will remain motionless, fastened together, dowel and groove, collision of harmony, motionless through distant time before the man, curving me backward, will raise my buttocks with both hands while we savor the feel of the swelling penis. After a time, he will draw back and begin a series of slow thrusting movements, driving deeper into the dark cave of my body. Rocking and moaning, he will drive deeper still, moving in time to the clenching of muscles, moving, moving, swaying together to a slow unhurried rhythm in the morning freshness of the drowsy island.

Waking, I clap my hands over my ears, for the Brahms Symphony Number Three is still playing outside my window, rising to a crescendo before offering a rare interlude of sweetness. The unexpected lyricism of the music sweeps me back toward the sensations of my dream.

A knot of fire. Quickly loosened before coming untied. A swift and powerful coupling. A rare experience, an experience never to be repeated, or else repeated as often as possible. I am not at all certain about the nature of this experience that, sleeping deeply, I have nonetheless undergone with frightening vividness.

A baby's shriek cuts across the serene lofty chords of the Brahms. I get out of bed. Wiping my body with a damp towel, I walk to the window and stand listening to the night music. I pull back the drapes. Across the space of the airshaft are the lighted windows of an orphanage. It is uncurtained, and I can see directly into one of the rooms. White walls and cupboards. Standing on a chair reaching inside the cupboard for something I can't see is a naked boy about twelve or thirteen. He stands on the chair for a long time. I can't see his head, only his body and one arm reaching inside the depths of the cupboard.

The baby's crying is louder. The Brahms continues: confident, poised, assured music. As I watch from the dark window, the boy standing on the chair slowly lowers his right hand, and his fingers encircle his penis. A smooth creamy-skinned child, he holds his penis for a long time in his rounded fingers. He does not move but stands motionless, his penis cupped in his palm. I stand motionless also, watching secretly as the small penis grows gradually stiff and the small hand that strokes it begins to play with increasing speed. I listen to the music of Brahms and watch the child's hand create his pleasure.

I cannot see the boy's face. He is standing still except for the moving hand and arm, standing on the white painted chair in the brightly lighted room with white walls and white wooden cupboards. The semen comes in several short jets, leaving the tiny organ slack and empty. With his free hand the child reaches in the cupboard, takes out a paper napkin and soaks up the fluid on his thigh. Then he takes a box of cookies out of the cupboard, jumps off the chair onto the floor and begins leisurely eating them one at a time, chewing methodically, then swallowing slowly, his tiny Adam's apple moving up and down his throat.

Without stirring, I stand watching. I catch my breath and hold it for several seconds, then laugh. The owner of the Brahms tape obviously rewinds it, because once again the insolent music falls upon the island's night air. A baby cries. The man and woman in the adjoining room resume their passionate dialogue.

Leaning out the window, I call into the darkness of the airshaft: "Please shut off that tape recorder."

But the Brahms continues.

Again, I call: "Stop! That's enough!"

Still, the heavy pompous music continues to assault me.

Mopping the sweat off my face, I lean far out the window and this time I shout:

"Stop playing that terrible music!"

As if controlled by the invisible hand of a demon, the music plays on and on. Exhausted, I fall onto my bed with my arms across my face. Without understanding why, I begin to cry.

The bull god was Dionysios. *Der Bulle. Il toro. O TauroS. Der Stier. El toro. Minotauromachie. Le taureau. El toro. Der Stier. Der Bulle. O TauroS.*

I wake up, clutching my shoulder for a moment before falling back among the damp sheets, horrified by this night, a night that seems longer than any I've ever before experienced, more menacing as well as more promising in a strange way I cannot understand. Reaching into the darkness, I turn on the bedside lamp, relaxing as the room fills with yellow light. It is an attractive room. I should be relaxing, not suffering. Rough-textured white walls. Heavy red drapes over the long windows. Dark wooden beams dividing the ceiling into squares of brown and white. There are even paintings copied from the frescoes at the Palace of King Minos; the women of the court are portrayed with their long curls cascading over their shoulders and flowing down their bare backs, women whose full round breasts are lifted high by wide golden girdles beneath which fall their graceful layered skirts of turquoise and scarlet cloth, skirts emblazoned with scalloped aprons of dark gold. Beautiful women, the women of the court of King Minos where once, long ago, Ariadne danced.

I tell myself that I am safer here than I was on the other island, in my small house perched on the rocks above the sea, a house where I lived for a while, alone. Lying back, I turn out the light and close my eyes, drawing the sheets up over my naked body.

But I still cannot fall asleep.

———————

Some months earlier, on a day that was radiant with light, my father died. A writer, he left an unfinished book, an unmade bed, and a small life insurance annuity to me, his only daughter. A painter and art teacher in a high school in New York City, I was desolate, or so I thought of myself. I was large and bony, saturnine. My mother died when I was seven, leaving me to the indifferent care of a stepmother, who died when I was twelve, in her turn, leaving me to the earnest but clumsy care of my father. He was an unsuccessful novelist who wrote twenty or twenty-five books. Only two were published, earning him altogether about $6,000. He was also a teacher, a part-time underqualified academic, who worked at night for a salary he was too embarrassed to talk about. Through one of his writers' organizations he obtained a decent life insurance policy, and this was his legacy to me, a chance to test—really to test—my talent.

Oh yes, my father drank heavily.

But there was always a chance, or so he thought, that one of his unpublished books might be successful, giving me an opportunity to live for five or six years in some distant magical part of the world where there were no adolescent students, pubescent boys and girls to disturb me with their giggles and their innocent smutty jokes. My unfortunate father had also been a homemade mystic of sorts, a lover of the poetry of Kabir. And so he had chosen his own epitaph, which read:

Listen, Friend, this body is his dulcimer.
He draws the strings tight, and out of it comes
the music of the inner universe.
If the strings break and the bridge falls
then this dulcimer of dust goes back to dust.

One day I folded a copy of my father's epitaph into my wallet, put my meager possessions in storage, packed my art supplies, my jeans and sandals, and boarded a plane for Rijeka, Yugoslavia. My destiny—an island called Korchula, which I had chosen on the flimsy basis of an enthusiastic recommendation from a good-looking man with whom I had had a brief affair. He said the island was both very beautiful and very cheap.

My style of painting was more surreal than anything else. Because I had too many paintings to take with me on the airplane, I was forced to put them into storage with my books and a few pieces of furniture. Deprived of my paintings, I made a list of their titles to take with me:

The Great New York City Blood Disaster in Times Square

Landscape at Sundown with Train Plunging into Sea

The Suicide Resurrected Through the Act of Love

Moonscape with Pregnant Cat Attended by her Tiny Physicians

Banquet at the Synagogue in Jersey City

The Great Los Angeles Tidal Wave Disaster (Shown with Gigantic Madonna)

Seascape with Male Nude and Flying Fishes

Lunch Among the Ruins of Modern-Day Macedonia

The Shopping Expedition Interrupted by Fellatio

All of these particular paintings were based on dreams, and all of my dreams were carefully recorded in my personal journal. So far I hadn't tried to sell or even display any of my work, because even though I loved some of the canvases, I was afraid that other people might laugh at them. But when I got to Korchula, everything changed. It was truly as though I had plunged into the depths of another world in which everything I looked at took on a strange luxuriant beauty.

Korchula is a massive thrust of volcanic rock rising out of the placid sea; it is covered with dark hemlock and cedar trees that in ancient times inspired the Greeks to call it "Korchula Negra." Grapevines wind around the hills, circling in and around the terraces of heaped-up rocks that keep the earth from washing down the mountain slopes into the Adriatic Sea. Everywhere I looked were fig trees spreading their shapely wide leaves generously loaded with the soft fleshy pink fruit from which the islanders took one of their names for woman's hidden sex.

After a short search I found a one-room house to rent, my haven, hand-cut from stones quarried right on the island. Inside, the walls were painted bright blue. The house contained a narrow lumpy bed covered with a sheepskin, a wooden table and two rickety chairs, a bureau, a gas plate, and an old stone sink worn smooth by time. Above the bureau

hung a writing Christ splayed against a Byzantine cross. Snatching this crucifix down, I stuffed it under a stack of towels in the bottom drawer of the bureau. To hide the stain on the wall where the effigy of the suffering man-god had hung I glued a photograph of the Minoan goddess of the serpents. Her bare breasts swelled above the wide girdle of gold. In her raised hands she held two twisting snakes. Perched on the goddess's crown was a cat, symbolic link to Bastet, who was sacred to the Isis cult of ancient Egypt.

For the first week or so I didn't even try to paint. I explored the island, walking up and down the narrow winding roads, grinning at the people I met, buying their eggs, their cheeses, their fruits and the heady wines they bottled themselves. I picked figs and tiny hard green apples. I gathered flowering branches and made bouquets in empty wine bottles. I walked and walked, exposing myself to the wind that blew steadily across the island at the same time every afternoon, blowing hot and steady, a hot plangent drying wind with a cutting edge and the power to cleanse everything it touched. I was not especially lonely at first because I had always been alone, and I was entirely captivated by the fresh simplicity of Korchula.

Sometimes, in spite of my youth, I felt as old and bent as a grapevine bowing to the ground, heavy with fruit. At these times I would stand in front of the strange wavy mirror above the stone sink and stare at myself. I expected to see a hag with coarse gray hair and a face like a nutshell. Instead, I saw a large flat sallow face wearing an expression of half-enchanted expectation. Something was going to happen to me here, but I didn't know what it would be. The important thing was that I wasn't afraid, though when I asked myself what there was to fear, I didn't have an answer.

Gradually, I began to make sketches and to write letters home. I tried to imagine sharing this house with any of the men I had known in New York. The wobbly chairs. The table with a gimpy leg. The straw mattress. Most men would be contempt-uous, or at least disapproving. The men I had known would need more sophisticated food than the cakes of soft, salty white cheese produced by the islanders and a wine more mature than the bitter *grk* which I was actually beginning to like.

Eventually, I started painting again. And something unexpected happened. Without my planning it, the work turned abstract. And the results, huge shrieks of color, were exciting. I was painting and I went on painting, imagining my concen-tration as a dark animal slithering through a long black tunnel, through a smoky hairy darkness that seemed to draw out my energy in bursts of color. I am painting, I muttered over and over. I am painting. I have been painting, will go on painting, shall paint, will paint, will have painted (some day). My own relentless productivity made me feel a little bit like a mule, and my loneliness began to feel like a strange form of ecstasy.

I fell in love with the wind. It was my only friend. The islanders sometimes tried to talk to me, even though they knew I couldn't understand their language. But there was the wind. Every afternoon I waited for it. I would pull my table outdoors so I could eat lunch under a tree; on my placemat, a newspaper, I arranged the soft white cheese, the bread and the sliced cucumber that were my usual fare, everything washed down with large quantities of bitter *grk*. And I suppose it was partly because of the *grk* that I would begin to feel excited a few minutes before the *Burra*—that was the wind's name— began to make his daily passage over the island. This wind was a definite presence—rough, hearty, reassuring in its regularity. The feel of the *Burra* on my body was like a caress edged with something savage. The breath of the *Burra* warmed my cheeks, sent my black hair flowing into the air, rippled up and down my arms like tongues of dry flame, coiled about my waist like the arm of a lover, and even licked its way between my thighs. Every afternoon I hurled myself into the arms of the *Burra*, longing for his rough embrace. Every day I rose to meet him, and every night when I fell asleep I savored the memory of this fragrant wind.

Often, after the *Burra* had departed, I would rest for a while, sitting on the rocks above the sea in front of my little house. I liked to perch on a flat stone with my arms clasped around my knees while I admired the view of the calm sea. I would try to empty my thoughts onto the warm stones, hoping that my mind would feel more spacious. I liked to imagine it hollowed-out, smooth as a bowl inside, molded by a gentle persistent hand into a clean waiting vessel. I was waiting. Meanwhile, I painted, and the works were accumulating so fast I was startled. Sometimes I worried about how I would get them back to New York. For the first time I began to imagine the possibility of living from the sales of my paintings.

One day when I was finished painting and was sunning myself, thinking about more or less nothing, a small boat entered the cove at the foot of the high rocks below my house. A man got out, tied the boat to a big rock, and began to climb the narrow stone stairway that connected my house and the sea below. I thought I'd seen him once or twice in the town. Or maybe I'd just passed him on the road. Was he the man whose shoulder I'd brushed when I was climbing up and he was climbing down the steps of a very old tower that stood on a nearby hill?

The man's approach was slow, hesitant, and almost respectful, as though he might be afraid of me, the strange foreign woman. A woven bag was swinging from his shoulder, and he was carrying something wrapped in a towel. Maybe it was a pig or a lamb. I stifled a giggle. It was the first time I'd laughed for so long.

Clambering up the rocks, the man gazed at me and crouched down while he unwrapped whatever he had in that towel. It turned out to be an enormous pink shell, a huge flawless Conch of Venus. Looking earnestly into my face, he offered it to me. The shell gleamed softly as if lighted from within.

A fisherman or a farmer, an ordinary island man. I stood up and stared at him, wondering whether he wanted to sell me the shell. In a rough way he wasn't bad looking. All the island men were handsome. Their bodies were carved lean by hard work and their skin darkened by the constant exposure to the sun. Many of these men had bright blue eyes resting under thick black brows, and their dark hair was usually wild and curly. However, I'd observed that even the young men's hands were ruined, permanently stained, the nails often broken and the fingers crooked and bent from the accidents of physical work. Because most of the islanders were younger than they looked, I didn't even try to guess my visitor's age.

But I noticed that his hands weren't damaged or dirty. They were well-shaped with long tapering fingers of the type called "psychic" by palm readers. The oval nails were very clean. The backs of his deft-looking hands were covered with silky black hairs. His eyes were a pale shade of gray, changeable, I noticed, depending on the light. Right now they were looking at me with an unmistakable glow of amusement that made me suspect I might be the object of some sort of joke.

When I felt sure that the Conch of Venus was intended for me, I smiled and thanked the man, rather hoping he'd just go away. Instead, he settled back on his heels, with an air of mischief on his face. He reached into the woven bag and took out a package wrapped in newspaper. This would be food of some sort, I thought, shaking my head. I didn't want to accept another gift from a man I didn't know, and anyway, he was undoubtedly a poor man. Seeing me hesitate, however, my visitor unwrapped the package himself, revealing a large yellow cheese and several slices of the dried pork the islanders called *prosciut*. There was also a loaf of crusty brown bread that smelled as though it had just been baked. The special treat, or so the man seemed to think, was a small bottle of rose-colored wine.

Yielding to a desire that seemed too forceful to deny, I sat back down on the rocks beside the stranger and allowed myself to share his food. When the sweet sugary liquor flowed into my mouth, I realized it wasn't wine but some sort of brandy. It made me think of the *Burra*. I liked it. And as I drank, smiling a little, the man was grinning. At first his face had been taciturn, almost gloomy, and so his smile was a shock. He had extremely white, perfectly formed teeth whose gleam was very brilliant in contrast to his black hair and tanned face. The condition of this man's teeth made me wonder what sort of work he did. Most of the islanders had missing or broken teeth. They often gestured toward their mouths, miming the question whether my teeth were real.

Reaching again into the same bag from which he had taken the food and brandy, the stranger lifted a long wooden flute. Perfectly contented, or so it seemed, he rested his weight on his heels, raised the flute to his lips and began to play a melody. The first notes seemed faltering, as though he were embarrassed by his own performance. It was a slow wandering tune, not at all like the lonely lament of the shepherd which I enjoyed late every afternoon, or the maddeningly insistent melody of the three-man bands that roamed up and down the roads playing gypsy dirges. These sounds seemed like sky-writing. They were languid and slow arabesques that coiled through the air. I felt as though I could glimpse them for a moment before they vanished, reappearing in pairs of ascending circles as the notes wound through the afternoon, binding my body with invisible cords.

The afternoon was unwinding. Later, that's how I remembered it. I sat with the man, drinking his rose-colored brandy. Eventually, I began to hear the suppertime cries of the animals. Cows calling for the hands that would relieve them of the warm milk in their swollen udders. Goats tossing their heads, making their bells tinkle. I heard the harsh clucking of women imitating chickens as they scattered the birds' evening corn.

Suddenly shattering this spell, the stranger jumped to his feet with a worried expression. He must have forgotten the time. Packing away his flute, he turned swiftly and, pointing at himself, repeated the name "Marinos" several times. I thanked him for the Conch of Venus, and Marinos sprinted down the stone stairway and leaped into his small boat. Before my eyes, he sailed away, disappearing around a bend in the cove.

His departure was very surprising. I was dazed, and I walked slowly back into my house. The sun was making a long gentle descent, and the dark green, almost black slopes of the island were darkening into geometric collages composed of shifting lights and shadows. For a moment I wondered whether I had fallen asleep and had been visited by a dream, a sweet haunting dream. But the Conch of Venus was real. I picked it up and cradled it in my arms as I went into the house, feeling like a serpent who had been charmed into a trance by a melody I hadn't even heard very clearly.

That evening I began to feel my loneliness like an ache. I turned on the radio, hoping for some simple music that would lengthen the mood of the afternoon. But all I could find was some boisterous polkas. It wasn't what I wanted, but it helped sustain my dreamy mood, and I listened while eating my supper of tomatoes, bread and cheese.

A few days later, the gray-eyed man came back again. This time it was nearly midnight when he arrived, knocking softly at the door. Deciding it was safe to invite him in, I opened the door, and there he stood, his arms filled with wildflowers. He laid them on the table and glanced around, eyeing my paintings with surprise. I didn't care what he thought of the paintings. I was more concerned about the fact that I was embarrassed by my nightgown. My visitor was wearing a rustic-looking suit. It was striped but only faintly, and he didn't look as ridiculous, I decided after surveying him for a while, as I had thought at first. He began talking to me in a language I didn't understand. It didn't sound like the Croatian native to the island. Nonetheless, to my surprise, I felt as though I understood what he was saying, even though I knew perfectly well I didn't. When he offered me some of his brandy (this one was amber instead of rose-colored), I shook my head. I was in a part of the world where a love potion wouldn't have been out of the question. Still, I sat down with him at the table. The open door at the man's back allowed the starlight to flow into the room. I couldn't believe it, but here I was in my nightgown, showing my paintings to a stranger whom I still felt uncomfortable calling "Marinos."

His responses to my paintings were appreciative. He nodded energetically and pointed at the ones he especially liked. For a long time we sat together, nodding and grinning at each other. And, once again, without warning, Marinos jumped up, sprang away and disappeared without an explanation.

When he was gone I recalled his wide tie covered with a blue flowered print. I fell onto the edge of my bed, laughing, I wasn't sure why. Was it really such a ridiculous tie? And what about my old-fashioned nightgown?

My paintings continued to burst into explosions of color as my hands moved, rapidly applying the paint to the Masonite boards. Sometimes I hated what I saw emerging under my hands, and then I started over, forcing myself to be patient as I slipped into the trance that went with work. Once in a while I fell asleep while I was working, nodded, dreamed, then woke up with a start and resumed painting again, as if I had never dozed off at all.

Marinos continued to make his visits, and little by little, we became friends. He told me he was not a Croatian but a Greek, somehow managing to explain that he was in hiding for political reasons he didn't make clear. I nodded and smiled, without for one minute believing him. I liked him but I didn't trust him because there was, nearly always, a certain look of mischief in his eyes that alternated with an expression of despair that I knew could disarm me.

As time passed, I found myself waiting for his visits night after night. We drank his homemade wines and brandies from my chipped jelly glasses. I always showed him the new paintings, and sometimes Marinos took them to the big town at the other end of the island and sold them for me.

Of course, eventually we became lovers. The stranger's nightly visits became the core of my days, inverting time, making of noon a midnight, of midnight a peak of light and intensity. Marinos made me feel soft and lazy. When we made love it seemed to me that I was swimming in a sea of gauze. He taught me that untutored hands can bestow subtle caresses, that whispered sounds need not be understood to express tenderness, that laughter can convey more ardent messages than words, that the body's love is most expressive when it is accomplished by the same powerfully focused concentration I brought to my painting. At times there seemed a touch of annunciation in Marinos's visits, annunciation, yes, but a pagan visitation.

And all this time I didn't for one moment believe that his name was Marinos.

One night we went for a late swim, picking our way down the narrow rock stairs as we listened to the waves rolling over the smooth shell of beach at their foot. The moonlight was very bright, nearly white, chilled by a cold radiance. Each sound seemed magnified, each scent intensified. A sharp cedar smell mingled with the perfumes of the wildflowers. The night seemed a huge soft lap into which we had tumbled to sleep for a while.

In the silver light I stood at the rim of the sea while Marinos took off his clothes: his jacket, the blue flowered tie, his white shirt and dark pants. I watched as he walked toward the sea, naked (he didn't wear underwear), stepped into the water and began to swim, raising one arm, inviting me to follow.

For a while I stayed on the shore, watching as he circled, playing, splashing, moving farther into the distance. A strange tug in my belly made me feel afraid, I didn't know of what. But finally I pulled my nightgown over my head, threw it on a rock, walked into the water, and began to swim after Marinos. The soft water made me want to yield to its depth, and I let myself be drawn farther and farther from the shore and deeper into the sea as I swam toward Marinos's moving body.

Together, we ploughed the sea. We swam, circling and splashing in the moonlight. I felt the power of Marinos's presence and was deeply contented. My fear disappeared. I turned onto my back, floating with my head pillowed on the water. I felt as though my entire body had become a swollen heart rising toward the bright cold sky.

We made love, then fell asleep, our arms wound around each other where we lay on the flat rocks beside the sea. When I woke up, Marinos was gone. He had returned to his boat, as usual, without a word of explanation, without a parting kiss, without a farewell, without a promise to return.

For days I waited for him to come back. I waited, unable to sleep, hardly able to eat, and worst of all, unable to paint. I roamed the island by day and lay awake at night suffering a nameless anguish.

Was it the anguish of abandonment?

Marinos did not come back.

Weeks passed. And still he did not come back. The gray-eyed man who had appeared so unexpectedly in his small boat had sailed away again while I offered my empty body to the violet light of the dawn.

Part 2

Ariadne was a vegetation goddess in Minoan Crete. Her name is derived from the words "very holy" or "very pure":

ARI HAGNE

Dances honoring her consisted of movements suggesting the twisting motions of the labyrinth.

At the sight of Divna, the flight attendants exchange glances. The male passengers raise their eyes over the tops of their papers and magazines. Alerted by the men's quick responses, the women also stare, some with hostility, others with a blend of envy and reluctant admiration. Divna moves toward her seat like an immense gorgeous ship attended by three tugs: her two curly-haired, golden-skinned children, and a slim handsome green-eyed young man.

Having slipped loose, Divna's hair electrifies her shoulders and back. Her white wrap-around dress is wet under the arms, and the strap of one of her sandals is broken. She feels sticky. As usual, she tells herself with instant forgiveness, she is a mess. Why is everyone staring, she wonders, before recalling that the messier she looks, the more people seem to stare at her. It's also because of her height and her bone structure; the European and American tourists who take this flight between Dubrovnik and Iraklion aren't used to seeing women who are as thickly upholstered with rosy flesh as Divna is. They stare as though she were a ripe piece of fruit.

Divna sighs as she edges her way down the narrow aisle, leading Tamara by the hand. She hopes that Bruno still has hold of Sasha and that he doesn't squeeze the boy's hand too tightly. Finally, the group of four are settled in their seats. Digging deep into her purple and gold woven bag, Divna searches for their passports and visas. She produces them: four dark red folders marked with stars. She hands these documents to Bruno and plunges her hand again into the tote bag, this time coming up with a special treat for the children, real Italian *Baci di Perugina*. She pats their reddish-golden curls and reaches once again into her bag, this time looking for her book, a collection of plays by Strindberg. The children suck their candy kisses and giggle. Divna opens the book.

Bruno gives her a dirty look. The man across the aisle is staring at her chest. Glancing down, Divna sees that her wrap-around has spread apart, exposing the ruddy nipple of one of her breasts. Just as she is about to pull her dress closed, Sasha reaches out and grabs her nipple in his fist. He gives it a sharp pinch.

"Sasha!" Laughing, Divna slaps the boy's hand.

Bruno gives her a rather disapproving look. Divna ignores this and gazes at him with admiration. He is tall, broad-shouldered, tanned and lean, with long legs. His head is covered with wavy brown hair, and his eyes are the same pale limpid green as the sea off the coast of his native Dalmatia.

Divna tries to read "The Ghost Sonata," but Tamara pulls her mother's loose hair.

"Mamma, they're talking about you!" exclaims the little girl with distress.

Listening, Divna hears a male voice say in French, "That's the actress, Divna Malkovich, or something like that. Some 'vich' or other. They all have those names. A magnificent animal, no?"

"Never mind." Divna pats her daughter's knee and hands her another *Baci di Perugina*. "Tamara, darling, we're all animals. People are animals too. There's nothing wrong with that."

And again she opens her book and tries to read. Divna didn't sleep well in Dubrovnik where she performed the previous night. The small town was crowded and noisy, bursting with tourists from all the nations of Europe and even Japan. There was a lot of tension and many outbursts. The other actors were Croatian and they disliked the Serbs in the cast. This included Divna. Though she tried to ignore the politics of the whole thing, she wasn't able to give her best performance because of her leading man's undisguised contempt. He seemed to look on her as a peasant overstuffed on corn and suckling pig. Fortunately, Divna was good natured. Otherwise, she might have driven her fist into her co-star's stupid arrogant face.

She closes her book of plays. It's impossible to read. Bruno is trying to persuade Tamara to trade places with him so he can sit next to her. She suspects him of wanting to claim her publically since word that she's an actress seems to have gotten around the plane. As Tamara and Bruno change places, Divna grins at the man across the aisle and offers him a candy kiss, which he accepts with an expression of childlike gluttony.

Divna opens her own *Baci* and unfolds the gooey little message inside. It reads: "Gentle words open iron gates."

She laughs as she pops the sticky soft chocolate onto her tongue. Since one of the things she wants to accomplish in Greece is to open certain gates in the heart of her estranged husband, Dionysios, she is gratified to have her strategy affirmed, even if only by an Italian manufacturer of chocolates.

Leaning near, Bruno whispers, "You shouldn't let Sasha touch your breasts the way you did a little while ago."

"I know." Divna stretches out her long brown legs and looks at her chipped pink toenail polish. It's from America and has the ridiculous name "Shrimp Toast," whatever that means. "Bruno, I didn't *let* Sasha touch my breast. It's not as though I *offered* him my breast. He reached out and grabbed it."

"It's indecent. If you let him do that, you'll make him neurotic. Do you want him to be as crazy as American men?

They're all in love with their mothers."

Briefly, Divna leans nearer and kisses Bruno on the lips. "What rubbish have you been reading?" Holding his head between her long golden fingers, adorned, like her toes, with Shrimp Toast polish, she cooes, "Don't worry, darling, Sasha won't be neurotic like an American. The next thing you're going to tell me, he'll become a homosexual because he loves his mother."

"I *also* love Sasha's mother." Bruno rubs his cheek against Divna's. "But I am not a homosexual."

"I guess not." Leaning back against the seat, Divna closes her eyes and tries to doze, but Bruno interrupts her, remarking:

"Your husband would be very angry if he knew you were going to Greece with me."

"He's used to not liking what I do."

"Divna, don't joke about things like that!" Bruno's face darkens momentarily.

"I'm not joking. The only thing he really worries about is that I might want to live with him again. He hates me."

"Oh, Divna, how can he hate you?"

"He can hate me because he is a Greek gypsy."

"The Greeks don't hate us because we're Slavs."

"That isn't what I mean. He hates me because I usually do what I want to do."

"You mean you *used* to do what you wanted to do—before you met me. Before you fell in love with me."

"Yes, of course that's what I said. I *used* to do what I wanted to do. But now...." Divna gives Bruno a playful smack. "Now I do what *you* want me to do."

She smirks; he looks away, then frowns:

"It's hard for me to believe that his name's really....Oh come on! It's not really Dionysios! That must be one of your stupid jokes."

Signaling the flight attendant, Divna orders milk for the napping children and ouzo for herself and Bruno. "A joke! Not at all; the name his mother gave him is Dionysios. Greeks like to name their children after gods. You know that. And why not? Guess what Dionysios wanted to name Tamara?"

"Venus? Something crazy like that?"

Sipping ouzo, Divna reluctantly gives up the idea of reading or even having a little nap. "About Tamara's name, 'Venus' is a good guess. My husband wants his daughter to be literary. He actually wanted to name her Sappho."

"My God! He really *is* a nut!"

The bus to Knossos jolts along the narrow dusty road and the passengers sit patiently enduring the bumpy ride. Dust blows up in flurries and flies in the open windows. The women sit with their knees slightly parted so they can balance the baskets and bundles on their laps. They hold babies, bags of grain, chicken with their feet tied together, jugs of wine, and brown paper bags containing jars of yogurt and all kinds of jam. Some of them grin at Miranda, and she returns their smiles; they have shared this route more than once. Without bothering to cover her mouth she yawns widely.

When the bus stops suddenly, the passengers lurch forward, are slammed back against their seats, righting their balance before they gather up their bundles and take their children's hands, climbing down the steep steps of the rickety bus. Miranda has barely set her sandaled feet on the ground when a mass of dark gray clouds sweeps across the sky, blackening the sun. There is a distant growl of thunder.

Miranda tells herself it makes no difference if there's rain. Knossos is a village strung along the road, a collection of cafés and shops offering souvenirs of the Palace. She can run for shelter in a café. Savoring the promise of a violent storm, Miranda walks jauntily toward the Palace grounds. Over her shoulder is a large bag which holds her sketchpad and an extra pair of sandals.

The ticket-seller grins at Miranda, winking as he squeezes her hand, with the same motion taking her drachmas. The man is wearing the native Cretan costume: a wide-sleeved embroidered blouse, pantaloons wrapped around his legs, soft slippers with bright embroidered toes, on his head a gold and red striped turban. His clothing is dirty and slightly ragged but he wears it with dignity.

As she walks toward the South Portico, Miranda looks at the Palace with an eye that captures something she'd never noticed before, and for a long time she stands in front of the two columns, studying their asymmetrical unity. They are like fraternal twins—the one a composition of square forms, the other of circles, stylized in the Minoan manner.

She sits down on a slab of warm stone and begins to sketch, but she is interrupted by a boyish voice:

"Hi! My name's Rudy. Aren't you staying at my hotel?"

She recognizes a boy of about fourteen whom she saw earlier at the hotel pool and in the curio shops along the harbor. He's a plump boy with a sexually ambiguous body, his buttocks high and protuberant. At a distance he could easily be taken for a girl the same age, or a little older.

"How do you like it here?" he asks.

"Oh, I love it!"

"I guess I'm interrupting you. I'm sorry."

"That's okay. Are you traveling alone?"

"Yes. Are you? Are you married?"

"No."

"I really like Greece! The people're very friendly."

"They seem to be friendly. And yet I haven't really made friends with anyone, have you?"

"Oh sure! This morning I met some really nice guys at a pastry shop."

"That's good."

"I'm going to go out with them later tonight. What're *you* doing tonight?"

"I don't know. I may just have dinner some place and go to bed early. It's not a good idea to get too friendly with people you don't know."

"That's what my mother'd say if she were here."

"Where is she?"

Rudy shrugs. "I don't know. See, I don't have a mother any more."

"I'm sorry. I must seem very nosy. But if I were your mother, I'd be worried about you."

"Would you really?" Rudy grins, but it seems a sad grin. "What about tonight? Maybe we could have dinner together."

With raised eyebrows Miranda answers, "I'll certainly think about it. Anyway, tell me....what happened to your mom?"

Rudy shifts from foot to foot. "She left. I don't know where she is. In fact, I don't really care where she is."

His defiant misery adds to Miranda's own sense of loss. "I'm really sorry. That's a shame!"

"No, it isn't. She was one hell of a terrible mother."

"Well, then, I guess it's good that she's gone."

Walking around the grounds, Miranda notices that the mute is coming toward them. She always sees him when she comes to the Palace in the daytime, a grotesque figure with a sprig of basil stuck above his ear and a fist full of wooden flutes that he tries to sell.

"Do you mind if I hang out with you for a while?"

"No, that's fine. I enjoy your company."

"Here comes the mute."

Grinning and burbling, he waves the flutes to attract their attention. Miranda has noticed that most tourists rush to open their wallets and shove drachmas into his dirty hand. They're in such a hurry to get away, they usually don't understand that they've bought a flute. This oversight makes the mute feel good because he's gotten the money without having to surrender one of the flutes he carves in the evenings, crouching in the dirt in front of his cardboard hut. Miranda often sees him carving while the shavings drift into a heap around his bare feet.

Thunder rolls. The humid air suddenly chills.

Rudy hands the mute some change and waves away the flute. But the mute lingers, watching Miranda sketch.

All at once the sun parts the dark clouds and comes burning into view. For a moment the landscape blazes with pink light.

The mute burbles with mysterious gaiety.

"Rudy, you never *did* tell me why you're traveling alone."

Lowering his eyes, he explains: "Well, see, my father's in New York. And we don't know where my mother is. So I came over here with my brother. He's two years older than me. First, we went to Mykonos. And Alex met some kids there. He divided up our money with me, and then he went to Turkey with these German kids."

"I see. So why didn't you go with them?"

"I don't know. I guess I just wanted to be on my own. So here I am."

A bus rattles down the road and jerks to a stop. A small group of islanders climb down and a family of four good-looking people attracts Miranda's eye: the father, a young man, a dark blond as graceful and sinuous as a tiger, the mother as stupendously proportioned as an animated caryatid, two plump rosy children sweet as Ruben's cherubs.

The storm breaks. Splinters of harsh red light streak the sky. Thunder blares. Huge drops of rain start to fall. Miranda pops the bag with her sketchpad under her skirt, ducks and makes a run for the thick woods that flank the Palace on one side. Both Rudy and the mute dash in the other direction toward Knossos.

She stands among the thick trees in the downpour, trembling, watching the rain splash against the earth. Gradually, she realizes that not far away a man is beckoning to her, wildly waving his arms. As her eyes adjust to the distance, she sees that this man is standing just inside the entrance to a cave. He must be a shepherd.

She sprints across the clearing and runs into the cave, finding herself one of a flock: six or seven sheep, two cows and an old man. He is tall and dignified in spite of his ragged shirt and the loose pants secured by a piece of rope. Above his long white beard the man's eyes are dark glittering brown. While Miranda thanks him for sharing his shelter, he shrugs repeatedly and waves his hands. Once in a while he murmurs soothing words to the sheep, though they don't seem nearly so terrified of the storm as the cows, who continually paw the floor of the cave.

Chilled air flows in from the clearing beyond. Miranda stands beside the shepherd, watching as lightning tears through the dark sky, again and again rending it with jagged spears. The old man seems surprised by the storm's fury; he shakes his head over and over again. Startled by a crack of lightning, he slaps his hands over his face.

Hoping to distract him, Miranda shows him her sketches but they are just a pulpy ink-stained mess. He smiles with resignation, seeming to ask, what can a person do against such a storm.

Gradually, the storm's intensity diminishes. The down-flowing sheets of gray water grow thinner, slightly more transparent, lighter, paler. The fresh smell of rain-soaked earth rises. Miranda waits a while longer; she likes listening to the voice of the old man as he soothes the animals.

Suddenly, he bends down, muttering. Miranda catches a glimpse of something gleaming in the mud. One of the cows has kicked up a metal object. Lying in the dirt near the cow's hooves is a bronze or dark gold metal plate or chain.

The old man kneels, picks up the object and scrapes away the dirt. He holds it up so Miranda can see it, but she doesn't know what it is: jewelry of some sort, a necklace maybe. In the center are two curved shapes. Could it be a Minoan relic? Maybe the peasants found valuable things all the time. Italian farmers working around the Etruscan tombs often find artifacts that they sell to the Department of Antiquities. Maybe the friendly shepherd has been lucky.

Thanking him for providing shelter, she starts to walk back across the archaeological site to the café where the bus stops. But the old man pushes the cow's discovery into her hands. It's for her. It's clear that he wants her to have it, and though she doesn't even know what it is, she senses that he would be insulted if she refused the gift.

She finally accepts it and stows it in her bag. She clasps the man's thin hand and pumps it up and down, thanking him over and over again. Taking off her sandals, she walks out of the woods through the wet clearing to the café.

When she gets there she's just in time to see Rudy hop onto the back of a motor scooter with a handsome older boy. As the scooter roars down the road, Rudy waves and yells something about "later tonight." The mute is still waiting for her, grinning and waving his flutes around.

Choosing a table near the magnetic family, Miranda orders

coffee. They're also having drinks while waiting for the bus to Iraklion. The golden-haired children have lovely oval heads. The rain has flattened their curls in stylized ringlets. The man's face, as well as his body, reminds Miranda of figures she's seen carved into the dull gold surfaces of antique coins. He looks like a Byzantine saint portrayed in an ecstatic trance.

The woman's profile, too, is arresting, every feature sharply chiseled in perfect balance with her other features. Her lips are full and shaped like a classic bow. Her large nose is straight and her enormous eyes are light brown warmed by bronze lights. She sits with her arms folded on the table. Her nipples are visible, straining against her white cotton dress as she bends across to wipe the rain from her children's faces.

Looking on, the children sip sodas. Their four tiny sandaled feet idly kick the rungs of their chairs. Giggling, they watch the two grown-ups.

Miranda feels the pain deep inside her belly grow, as though there is a creature inside: mute, imprisoned, sighing from a nameless fluttering anguish.

"Magnificent, no?"

The waiter's remark startles Miranda. Thinking of the man, she replies: "Yes, magnificent. Who is he?"

"He?" The waiter stares at her in disbelief before bursting into laughter. "Not *he*! *She*! She's a well known actress."

"And her husband? Is he an actor?"

"Him!" The waiter twists the ends of his long mustache while he makes Miranda wait for his answer. "In a way, maybe he's an actor. He's her man, at least for now. Probably, he has to perform well to keep her entertained." He pounds his bulging stomach and guffaws.

Aware that she's probably setting herself up for the waiter's ridicule, Miranda nonetheless fishes for more information: "He looks like an artist of some type."

"*That* guy!" the waiter jeers. "He's nobody. He's just an ordinary guy."

"Ordinary?"

"You probably think that guy's good looking." He laughs loudly. "Listen, where he comes from, all the men look like him and lots better."

At this moment the bus comes careening down the road causing a flurry of activity among the café's customers.

Quickly downing her coffee, Miranda pays up and hurries out to the road with the others.

Later in the evening she walks along the curving beach at the tip of the island beside the breakwater. Beyond the wall lies the sea, a hot and churning sea that is sometimes turbulent and sometimes calm, but always slightly threatening. Earlier, she tried to call Rudy to accept his invitation for the evening, but he wasn't in his room, and she didn't find him at the pool either. And so, she is going to have another lonely evening.

She comes to a waterfront café with huge pale blue dolphins leaping across its whitewashed façade. Inside, the walls are decorated with fishnets filled with sponges and large shells, colored balls, and dried starfish. The wooden tables and chairs are covered with red cloths. Candlelight throws shadows of flame against the walls. As she sits down, Miranda feels oddly excited; the air seems to vibrate with unheard music, the earth to float on an amber sea.

Through the open door of the restaurant Miranda hears the sea slapping steadily against the stone breakwater. The air is salty, still fresh from the afternoon's storm. When she begins to eat her salad of cucumbers and olives, the beautiful family arrives.

Divna tries to slip into the chair that will give her the best opportunity to admire a handsome man sitting near the door, but Bruno outwits her, forcing her into a chair that faces the back wall of the restaurant. Divna is forced to admire, instead of the man, soaring dolphins and ornamental fishnets. Pretending to help her into the chair, Bruno pinches her arm.

"Stop that!"

"Don't stare at that guy! You're with me!"

"I guess I am!" Grudgingly, she changes her gaze. "Bruno, if you don't stop pinching me, I'm going to slap you!"

The protest in his mother's voice makes Sasha glance at her, alarmed. But Divna smiles and chucks the boy under the chin. "It's all right, Sasha. Aren't you hungry, darling?"

She stares glumly at the painted dolphins. Bruno's possessiveness has become too irritating to put up with. She sits quietly, one hand buried in Sasha's curls, the other on Tamara's shoulder. Tomorrow she will begin a month-long separation from the children while her husband takes them to visit his family, his mother on Korchula, his father and wife in Athens. Without her children, she reflects, she will feel as solitary as the sad-looking woman across the room.

Bruno orders grilled fish, tomato, onion and parsley salad, bread, and fruit. Distracted by her covert study of Miranda, Divna doesn't even notice when Tamara steals her wine and drains the glass.

Bruno snatches it from the child. "Divna, you're going to have a drunk kid. What's wrong with you?" He delivers the reprimand in a low, controlled voice, and for a few seconds, Divna stares at him as though she doesn't even see him. She struggles against an impulse to tell him he can pack his bag tonight, as far as she's concerned. But if she gives in to this anger, she'll be alone in Greece, truly alone for the entire time of the children's visit to their father.

Sasha whimpers: "Mamma, Mamma, make the food come soon. I'm starving!"

"Yes, darling, that's what a mamma's for, to make the food come."

Bruno's expression is gloomy as he sips wine but as soon as the plates of fish are placed on the table, he seems more cheerful. He bones the children's fish.

After all, he *is* kind to them, Divna reflects. He puts up with a lot from the children, *her* children. They demand so much time and attention, and she sometimes loses patience with them.

Miranda notices that Strindberg's *Dream Plays* is sticking out of the actress's handbag.

A gypsy with a candle in her hand is approaching Miranda's table, swaying her wealth of flounced skirts.

"Lady, Magda wants to tell your future. Okay?"

As she watches Magda approach the dark woman, Divna has an urge to ask the gypsy to read cards for her too. But it will just spark another fight with Bruno, and somehow she lacks energy for it. Her mood is close to despair and yet she also feels anxious. An idiotic impulse tempts her to interpret the afternoon's storm as bringing bad luck, as if nature would produce a storm just to give *her* a message, she, an insignifi-

cant actress. And a fool! If Aunt Mileva were here, she'd remind
Divna that she's only a peasant girl with a remarkable talent
for which not she, but God deserves credit.

Seen close up, the gypsy isn't as old as Miranda thought at
first. She has a smooth oval face and tilted black eyes that
express a kind of defiant confidence. Her hands are smooth and
soft, and as they move, shuffling and laying out the Tarot
cards, her jewelry makes music. She digs a crumpled pack of
cigarettes from her pocket and offers Miranda one.

"The past," Magda begins. "Not so much bad. Dull maybe.
Hmm. There's a man, who....No. It's not him.

What happened when you were....?"

Tamara slumps forward, asleep in her chair. Sasha sways
toward his mother's arm, clutching her shoulder. Divna reaches
out and removes the napkin tucked in her son's collar.

"I'd like to stay for the music, Bruno."

"Whatever you want, darling," he concedes, bending toward
her with a seductive smile.

"A gift," Magda continues. "Did something new come to you?
Someone give you something?"

"Yes."

"What?"

Miranda hesitates.

"Don't want to hurt you. Something to wear, yes? No?"

Miranda takes the metal object from her bag and shows it to
Magda, who brings it close to the candlelight and squints at it.
Without comment, she lays it on the table, studies the cards
she's arranged in a circle, and asks:

"What is your name?"

"Miranda."

"This name have special meaning?"

"Yes, it's the name of a girl in a play by Shakespeare."

Magda nods as if a suspicion has been confirmed.

"Something very unusual going to happen to you, lady."

At Miranda's glance of alarm, the gypsy pats her hand. "No worry. You a very shy person. I think you have never yet been in love."

"I was, but the man—"

"I know. He went away from you. That is not unusual."

They laugh before Miranda asks: "What's going to happen to me?"

"It will change your life."

"Does it have anything to do with a man?"

The gypsy laughs bitterly. "Can a woman's life have a deep change without a man in it somewhere?"

"Will it hurt me?" Miranda whispers.

"Hurt, no. Frighten, yes." The gypsy leans back in her chair and smiles. "Try be calm, whatever happens." Again, she raises Miranda's gift to the light, examining it at arm's length. She taps it here and there and pushes it into various shapes. It unfolds and is transformed into a circle with curved horns forming a peak in the middle.

"Is it a crown?" Miranda asks. "It looks like a crown."

Nodding, Magda places the crown on Miranda's head. But she snatches it off and buries it again in the bottom of her bag. Her heart is crowded with dread.

Music explodes in the small restaurant. During the gypsy's reading, musicians had been assembling their instruments:

guitar, drum, accordion, and horn. With the players is a woman who seems herself a fifth musical instrument. Throwing
back her head, she gives a harsh fierce cry, drawing all eyes to
her vivid figure. She is a compelling image—gaudy, magnetic,
glittering with bright colors and gold jewelry. A shiny-textured
bright pink skirt, a matching bolero, a blue and gold striped
blouse with wide fluffy sleeves. Everywhere, the woman seems
adorned with gold: around her waist a gold mesh belt, several
gold necklaces hanging from throat to stomach, on her head a
cap of gold coins. Beneath the cap of gold, waves of black hair.
The gold coins that hang from her cap adorn her smooth forehead like beads glittering at the ends of thin golden threads.

For a moment she stands quietly in front of the musicians,
waiting for the resonance of her exuberant shout to fade into
silence, standing with a forefinger against her lips, exuding
energy, an abandoned, almost ecstatic happiness. Against the
background of the four musicians, the woman bursts into song.

Sasha and Tamara quickly straighten up in their chairs,
rubbing their eyes. Before the song ends, Divna jumps up and
applauds wildly.

Miranda is also stirred by the boisterous music. It is tough,
assertive, festive music that demands a response in the same
mood, but this response eludes her. The music disturbs her
slightly, cutting through her solemn haze of brooding melancholy expectation.

The restaurant is filling up with people: couples, families
and groups of tourists at every table and in every chair. Among
the crowd are Rudy and some older boys. Soon, the Dolphin
Café is packed. The people stamp their feet in time to the
music, snap their fingers, tap their toes on the floor.

As the music plays on, people get up to dance. Whooping and stamping, throwing back her head, the gypsy sings, crying out now and then to punctuate the melody with unrestrained happiness. The actress drags her man out of his chair and draws him into the dance. It isn't a movement for couples but a line dance in a convoluted form created by a chain of people placing their hands on the shoulders of the person ahead. In a long snaking line, the dancers weave through the restaurant, gliding deftly around and between the tables in a continuous serpentine motion.

Miranda is inspected by several men who seem to wonder about asking her to dance, but she refuses to make eye contact with any of them. The effect of the wine, the powerful music, the wild sounds of horn and drum, make her feel prim and isolated, totally alone. She broods on the gypsy Magda's prophecy and she also yearns for a dancing partner, for a welcoming hand to draw her out of her chair and into the line of swaying dancers.

But unhappiness, Miranda notes with bitterness, does not attract dancing partners. She is too shy to let anyone choose her.

The small café vibrates with happiness. But nobody asks Miranda to dance. Her pain grows. She cannot be an uninvolved observer any longer. Quickly, she flees, escaping alone into the night.

Divna wakes up, laughing. She squirms but can't move far because Bruno's leg lies across her thighs. They had fallen asleep with the light on. In the mirror opposite the bed she can see their entwined bodies. And again, she laughs, more softly this time because she doesn't want to wake up Bruno. For a second or so she looks at him with ironic tenderness, then turns her face up toward the ceiling while she recalls the ridiculous dream that caused her laughter.

She was in the apartment she shares with Aunt Mileva in Beograd, when a woman burst out of the bedroom closet. She was a stout middle-aged woman dressed entirely in black: black dress, black apron, black stockings, and old-fashioned black lace-up shoes. On the woman's head, a black babushka. When she popped out of the closet, Divna ran at her and tried to shove her back inside. The woman resisted, however, and Divna beat her, pounding the tightly corseted body with her fists. But the older woman was tough. Divna's fists made no impression on her. Even though she struggled as hard as she could, Divna couldn't shove the black-swathed woman back inside the closet. She possessed an energy that seemed superhuman, and even Divna, with her considerable strength, hadn't been able to force the specter back into hiding.

For a while she lies quietly, sucking on her fingers as she used to do when she was a child and hadn't yet learned to use her mouth for talking. Knowing that she can't go back to sleep, she decides to get up and go for a walk. Slowly disengaging from Bruno, she slips out of bed. Putting on a loose red dress, binding it with a woven cord, she sweeps her hair up inside a gold scarf and ties espadrilles around her ankles. She cuts a thick slice of bread, eats it quickly, puts a bottle of brandy to her lips, drinks deeply, and packs both bread and brandy into a basket.

After checking on the sleeping children in the adjoining room, Divna leaves the hotel, crossing the wide area where the swimming pool is located. It is flooded with light. If Bruno were to wake up and look out the window, he'd see her walking away from the hotel toward Knossos.

As she passes the pool she hears a sound like a long sob, a choked smothered cry. Pausing, she searches the shrubs and trees around the pool. There is a crackling in the bushes. Maybe someone's hiding in there. Maybe someone needs her help. Divna pauses, wondering whether she should search further. But if she lingers around the hotel, Bruno may see her and come to the wrong conclusion about why she's slipping away in the middle of the night.

"Who's there?" she whispers loudly. If an answer comes, she'll go on searching. But the only response is a silence that reminds Divna of a breath exhaled over an inconceivably long interval. Her uneasiness grows; she feels certain that nearby someone is suffering, maybe lying in the bushes in pain. It's wrong of her to leave and yet it seems dangerous to stay.

Again, she whispers, "Who's there?" And again the only response is an eerie silence. With a shrug she looks up at the pale bright sky. So much moonlight can make people crazy. She feels a tension greater than any she has experienced since the last time she saw her husband. She has a characteristic (she calls it "tenacity" when she likes herself and "stubbornness" when she doesn't) that prevents her from compromising, even to hold a lost love. And for a moment or so she laments the mutual pride that shattered her marriage into unreconstruct-ible fragments.

In the moonlight, the road unfurls like a ribbon of tinsel flowing toward Knossos with a brilliance that soothes her. She walks along, humming, giving no outward sign of her distress. After all, she's had a lot of practice at being people other than herself. She knows that any stranger who might see her now as she walks along the road in the moonlight, her mouth still tasting of dark brown bread and her tongue still smarting from brandy, would take her for a peasant rounding up stray chickens.

Peering into the landscape that lies silently reclining in a blaze of opal light, Divna swings along the road, preparing for the difficult morning when she will have to face the man she once adored in order to bargain like a market hag for their children's time. It is the demand for control where there had once been wildness, the necessity for business-like behavior when they ought to have been either shouting at each other or snorting and hooting. It is this unnaturalness that disturbs her.

To combat this mood, she begins to whistle one of her husband's most popular songs, "Sinfonoula," a parody of military pomposity. But suddenly she lowers her head and walks more slowly, recalling how she had felt when she and Dionysios had created the children they were now fighting over. This man once had been able to make her feel as though he had reached inside her body to stroke her heart with tender fingers.

But that was a long time ago.

She goes on whistling "Sinfonoula," giving herself a shake mentally for even thinking about this man who doesn't love her any longer, the husband she drove away by being fierce and independent and unyielding. Maybe she was too young when she married him. Maybe now that she's more mature, considering the men she's known since her separation, and the extensive love-making she's experienced, maybe now she'd know how to value the man whose once-rapturous love she had been too foolish to protect.

Divna whistles even louder. Gazing to the right, then to the left, she admires the luminous earth and hills lustrous with moon milk, a beauty that is compelling but cannot assuage her nervous grief. Bitterly, she tells herself that she will never again be loved by a man as fine as the man she has already lost.

When she arrives at the Palace and walks across the glittering plane of moonlight, Divna begins to feel chilled, as if she has been struck by the icicles of the moon, splashed in starlight. She feels slightly sick, and as she pauses for a moment, pressing her ribcage to suppress the heaving in her belly, she wonders whether she should go right back to the hotel. She is standing in a pool of moonlight near the two pillars on the south porch of the Palace. In the past, the sight of such unrepentant beauty would have comforted her, but tonight she's the victim of a pain too strong to be cured by beauty. She will have to discharge this pain in a frenzy of physical activity. She will dance herself back to calmness at least, if not to health.

As she walks toward the area of the Palace called "Ariadne's Dancing Platform," she stops, startled. She is not alone here. Sitting in the shadows at the edge of the dancing floor is another woman.

"Who's there?" Divna calls into the night.

As she continues forward, she sees the woman trembling.

"Who's there?" Divna calls again. Now she recognizes this woman as the same one who, last night, had sat gloomily alone at the Dolphin Café, refusing to dance, stubbornly defending her isolation.

"I couldn't sleep," Miranda replies. "So I came out here to get away from my hotel room."

"I remember you. Weren't you at the Dolphin Café?" Divna sits down on a chunk of shattered column, knees wide apart. With a supple motion, she pulls off her scarf, freeing her hair to tumble around her face in frenzied curls.

"You look like a goddess," Miranda says, "like a statue freed from her pedestal."

Divna smiles to herself. "People say things like that sometimes." Opening her basket, she takes out the bottle. "How about some brandy? It'll help you sleep when you go back to your room."

"If I ever *get* back to my room. But, why not?" Miranda drinks deeply from Divna's bottle. "Isn't this funny? Here we are, two strangers, sitting in the moonlight together."

"Shall we dance?" Divna quips. "Isn't that what someone from your country would say in this situation?"

"You've been watching old American movies." Miranda hands the brandy bottle back to Divna. She stares across the dancing floor.

"Some archaeologists say this was the dancing platform that Daedalus built for the real-life Ariadne."

"I believe it is. That's why I came here." Unwinding the braided belt from her waist, Divna repeats, "Now I know why I came out here really. I want to dance. Would you like to dance too?"

"Maybe. Well, why not?" Miranda stands up and takes one end of Divna's belt in her hand.

"It's easy. It's a serpentine dance. Turn to the left, always to the left. I'll chant. Listen. It's really easy."

Divna begins to move, hurling her head forward and backward as she chants a simple two-syllable word, always heavily accenting the first syllable, chanting clearly as she moves with strongly articulated steps, weaving across the light-flooded space.

Miranda easily follows, bound to Divna by the rope in their hands, following each other, Miranda wheels and turns, the dance steady, measured by the beats of the chant. The women spin and wheel, spiraling back again as they turn. Turning and wheeling in the bright light, the women create patterns by their spinning bodies.

Patterns on the dancing floor: reverberations of the goddess Ariadne, Ariagne, Aridela, she who was born of the sea, worshipped in Greece as Aphrodite, in Rome as Venus, in Egypt as Isis, and here on this island of Crete as Ariadne, princess and priestess, bride of the sea, queen adorned with the crown of Thetis, abandoned by mortal man, she was rescued, to become the bride of the god who is called "the one who comes," the "stranger" god, the god from the East, Dionysios.

The two women hold the rope in their hands and dance together, spelling out an invisible melody in the moonlight. Heads thrown back, they dance with their eyes raised to the sky where—soon—a disk of orange fire will appear.

Dionysios wakes from a deep sleep with a start, quickly, painfully, and he tries to recapture the dream that has already eluded his mind—the dream with its power to sweep him far beyond this world toward another world where pain is submerged under an avalanche of narcotic imagery.

He's lying in the bottom of a boat on a pile of tarpaulins, making an illegal entry into his own country. He massages his wounded right wrist with the fingers of his left hand, but even this slight pressure causes more pain. If only he could sleep, if only it were not such a bright night glaring in the hostile moonlight, the light itself attacking the night, which should always be dark and soft and welcoming, like the inside of a woman's body. He blinks to shut out the steely moonlight. He curls up, pulls a piece of canvas over his head, and tries once again to sleep.

When the moon is full and the hills are glittering silver, the women dance together. Feeling the energy rise as they wheel and turn, sketching spirals on the dancing floor of the daughter of King Minos, the doomed and favored priestess Ariadne, Ariagne, Aridela, priestess of the labyrinth. As they dance the women hold writhing serpents, arms upraised, in both hands, serpents twisting while the women weave in the moonlight, circles spinning from left to right, reversing direction, turning from right to left and left to right, reversing again, the women's bare feet stamp the earth floor of the dancing area as they circle and twirl, arms aloft, in their upraised hands the serpents, sinewy, coiling, writhing and uncoiling, reversing spirals of creation, spirals of destruction, webs of rhythm spun on bare feet of dancing women, feet that turn and glide over the earthen floor of Ariadne's dancing platform, center and heart of the sacred site of Minos. Twirling and spinning the patterns of the sacred dance, the hearts of the women catch fire and blaze with ecstasy.

The wind shifts. The small boat rocks sharply. The man asleep under the tarpaulin wakes up and stares at the bright sky in which the moon seems as flat as a child's cut-out. He rubs his wrist and sighs. He is so tired! And he wanted to be at his best when he saw Divna again, not so much to attract her as from pride; certainly, she will be displaying one of her fashionably-dressed lovers, some ass, an oversexed boy done up in the latest styles from Rome.

Why, he asks himself, is he waiting to divorce this spoiled peasant? Because of her extraordinary talent, Divna has always had everything she wanted, including himself and the better part of his youth. When he tried to persuade her to become part of a couple, Divna had rebelled with alarming force. Even her own aunt admitted that no one had ever succeeded in controlling Divna. And he, who had never before encountered this tenacity in a woman, had given in to Divna, whose fair coloring and heroic stature were deceiving, giving the impression of girlish charm and placidity.

In reality, Divna was more like a volcano in full eruption. She did whatever she wanted to do when she wanted to do it. This total liberty was, *she* thought, the reward life gave her for her ability to tear people's emotions from their clenched throats and to cause sobs to burst from tightly closed lips. Divna seemed convinced that her gift for arousing deep emotions in others gave her a license to be utterly and wholly herself at all times, a rare privilege. His mother is the only other person Dionysios has ever known who is as totally in possession of herself as Divna. But Esma has won this freedom, not been born to it, like Divna, who is blessed with vast natural energy. Like Divna, Esma also has a gift for repeated acts of successful rebellion, but she is not intimidating.

Nonetheless, he has to admit Divna does bow to two forms of discipline: the demands of her work and those of motherhood. Dionysios was relieved when he saw that Divna, who rejected her obligation to fulfill his needs, was by nature sensible about their children, not only loving them with uninhibited ardor, but also caring for them with innate common sense. Not that Divna devoted great amounts of time to mothering; it was more that her instincts were sound. She loved Tamara and Sasha with a genuine affection that seemed free from the sense of pride that inspired her never-ending rebellion against him.

Her arrogant insouciance at first puzzled him and later enraged him. There was obviously no way he could force his wife to love him as he wanted, needed to be loved—wholly, attentively, tenderly, even passionately. But the intensity, that to him meant passion, seemed to frighten Divna who, early in their marriage, responded with a naturalness that seemed promising and that he had tried to ignite to a more incendiary expression. But after their children were born, Divna began to seem alarmed, even threatened by her own sensuality, the more so by his capacity to arouse her. Eventually, Divna began to avoid his caresses and to openly admire other men in the streets or in cafés, even when Dionysios was with her. She began to meet his love-making with a brusque and insulting selflessness, encouraging him to spend himself quickly without regard for her pleasure, an attitude that less affectionate men might have greeted with relief. But it depressed and saddened him, even though he knew it was just her way to remain free.

She seemed to have little tenderness and no passion left for him, and her demanding career consumed her time with rehearsals and tours throughout the Balkans and Europe.

Finally, he had shaped a silent and secret farewell to Divna, living with her only part of the time while he began the process of emotional separation. Whatever the source of Divna's aloofness, he knew he would never receive a more generous portion of the love she began to bestow lavishly upon a growing world of admirers and aspiring lovers who clustered around her like worshippers at the feet of an immense and indifferent Aphrodite.

To Dionysios his wife seemed less a woman than an embodiment of energy, a law unto herself, and though he turned to other women casually, seeking consolation, diversion and sexual expression, he had focused the greater part of his largely unused, almost wasted passion in telling the world about the latest and most brutal abuses of power by bureaucrats and power-brokers around the world. Composing and performing music became his passion, and he began to direct the major portion of his energy to writing satirical songs that he performed in various European cities.

Very soon he developed a reputation as a singer with an ugly but "interesting" voice and a large original repertoire. In a bright blue wooden trunk in his mother's house on an Adriatic island, he kept the musical compositions he was working on and wanted to complete as soon as he could get everything settled with Divna. Until then he would drift around Europe like the gypsy he was—at least on his mother's side—singing his derisive songs in a harsh passionate voice.

The strange thing was, this vagabond life, at which he was almost effortlessly successful, didn't really suit his temperament at all. Even though he was far more his mother's child than his autocratic Greek father's, Dionysios harbored a secret yearning for an orderly life, for the routine of sleeping at night with a woman curled up beside him, of ardor and sensuality. He was not ashamed to dream of a tender love lived out simply in a small house on an island where he would have plain food to eat, a deep clear sea in which to swim, and from dawn to twilight, a breeze laced with the scents of flowers.

But even his mother hadn't been able to create a simple life. Even though she was entirely independent not only of his father but also of all other men, she had bought this independence by shaking a tambourine and her gypsy skirts in all the nations of the Balkans and Southern Europe. Apparently, he was just like his mother, destined to endure the life of tedious wandering that characterizes a mediocre entertainer, at once glamorized and tainted by gypsy blood.

Exhausted, he lies back in the small boat and pulls the tarpaulin away from his face, allowing the cold starlight to chill his stiff body with radiant indifference.

When the moon is full and the fields are glittering with stalks of silver grain, the women dance. They pace, whirl, and pound the earth with their bare feet. As the women whirl and turn, they cry out, making short eerie passionate noises, women's bodies swaying with a single obsessive motion, harsh voices crying.

"Aiye! Aiye!" they shout, flinging back their heads and shaking their raised fists as though holding up writhing serpents; twisting to the same rhythm, their feet are pounding into the earth as they move, spelling out a chant with their stamping feet and their rough voices that cry out in the moonlight.

Arms folded under his head, Dionysios rests in the rocking boat and listens to the throbs of pain in his body as he stares up at the light that is slowly widening in the sky above him. Growing fainter now, the stars are blending into the pale gray mist of the approaching dawn. In the vast overhead space of violet-tinged emptiness, the moon lingers like a pale fruit, swollen with cold light and dark craters of ice, the moon which Dionysios has always hated. Instead, he has habitually turned toward the sun, seeking it with a frozen bird's desperate desire for warmth. Even in Greece he has never gotten enough sunlight.

He wants to take his children to Korchula for a month or so, to his mother's house, but first he'll visit his father and his stepmother in Athens. These days will be sad. He doesn't like or respect his stepmother, and he and his father have been uneasy enemies ever since Dionysios was a child and discovered his natural mother, the wild gypsy Esma.

When Esma was twelve, she was raped among the rocks along the coast of an island by his father, who was vacationing there. Esma had given birth to a boy whom she named Dionysios. For a while she raised him herself, teaching him to sing and dance, encouraging him to be a little savage who was comfortable in the water and in the woods. He could swim as well as a baby seal.

But when he was about four years old, his father had claimed him, forcing Esma to give him up. From that time on he was raised by his father and his young wife, Electra, who

could not have any children. Dionysios's father had renamed
him "Marinos." Without a family to protect her, with no one but
a ragged band of gypsies to defend her right to her son, Esma
was helpless. Compelled to leave the island's gypsy camp,
Dionysios had gone to live in a big white house perched high
above the sea.

His stepmother tried to love him, but he was much too dark
to suit her ideal of a son. Electra, who was half French, was
slim and fair, entirely un-Greek in appearance. Finally, his
father had hired a nursemaid to take care of him. He almost
never saw his father, who traveled around the world
accumulating money. And he almost never saw Electra either.
She took long trips to France, returning with bags full of
dresses, shoes, hats, handbags, and dozens of expensive toys
for him to play with. When she was at home, Electra spent her
days exercising and bathing and making herself up for the long
dinner parties at which she sat quietly beside his father,
dressed in expensive fabrics, perfumed and adorned with gold
and pearls, as useless as a toy. As for the nursemaid his father
had hired, she was a crabby Swede who got fat on the jellied
Turkish candy they called *ratluk* and on Turkish coffee laced
with ouzo. She didn't learn to speak Greek.

Once when the family went to Korchula for the summer,
Dionysios received a shocking surprise—an unannounced visit,
more like a visitation, from a girl with curly black hair and eyes
that alternated between a savage glitter when she looked at
Electra and a gaze of shy love when she looked at him.

Until he ran away to visit her when he was twelve, Dionysios
did not know that this gypsy girl was his mother. He knew only
that a singer named Esma sometimes visited him—always
secretly—when he was playing on the bone-white rocks high

above the brilliant blue sea. Esma brought him gifts: a wooden flute, a tern's egg, the curly-haired skin of a white lamb, and a tambourine with red, green and purple ribbons streaming from its bells. Esma warned him to keep these gifts hidden. She said that Electra would be very angry if she found out that Esma had discovered a way to visit him when he was playing alone, the Swede having been lulled into a torpid nap by generous portions of ouzo and sunlight. And then, the gypsy warned, Electra would tell the boy's father, who would find a way of frightening Esma into staying far away from the big white house where her son lived with a blonde foreigner and a man whose claim to fatherhood was rape.

This was the reason that Esma, many years later when she had saved enough money to buy a house, had chosen to live on Korchula.

Lying limp and exhausted in the cool light of the latent dawn, Dionysios thinks about the strangeness of his origin and the one constant—more or less constant—figure in his unpredictable broken life, Esma, his mother.

Side by side, the two women walk away from the Palace, as they head for the road to Iraklion, leaving behind a pool of shadows, Ariadne's dancing floor.

Placing her hand on Miranda's shoulder, Divna remarks: "We're nearly the same size."

"In my country big women are considered ugly."

"Not in mine. We're just as big as the men. I can do the same work as any man."

"Do you *want* to do the same work as any man?"

"Of course not! But it makes me feel good to know that I *can* do it if I have to."

Miranda laughs, swinging her arms.

Violet light spills onto the narrow winding road, flooding it with a delicate haze. The waking birds are beginning to sing fragile tentative phrases as meaningless as the preliminary exercises of singers. The air is still cool and fresh, scented with wild basil.

"Let's have some more brandy." Divna plunges her hand into her basket and emerges with the bottle. "New friends should always drink together."

As Miranda sips, allowing the rough yet sweet taste of the brandy to linger on her tongue before swallowing it, she recalls how, on that other island in that nearby country, she had recklessly agreed to drink rose petal brandy with a strange man who had visited her unexpectedly, had gradually and subtly become her lover and had, just as unexpectedly as he had appeared, one day disappeared.

Walking along the road to Iraklion with a strange woman,

Miranda thinks about this man whom she had allowed herself to embrace during the sultry nights of Korchula's summer and whom she had allowed nearly to destroy her with his abrupt and cruel abandonment. She had been tricked by the man's disguise of good-natured simplicity. Consequently, she had been seduced and abandoned—for all the world like the pitiable hand-wringing victims of old-fashioned melodramas.

"Have you ever been in love, *really* in love?" Miranda suddenly asks her companion.

"Oh, I don't know. Maybe once." Divna glances at the watch strapped to her wrist by a wide band. "Once, I think. But I was too spoiled to make it last."

"Spoiled?"

"Not by money. We are a poor people. I was spoiled by early fame."

"Fame?"

"Yes. I'll explain that."

Divna stops and gasps. Lying in the road coiled, ready to strike, is a large brown snake. The creature stares at the women with apparent indifference.

"Don't scare him," Miranda warns. She kneels in the road, groping in her bag for something Divna can't see. Bending forward, Miranda offers the serpent a piece of leftover honey-soaked pastry that she'd taken from the Dolphin Café to eat later. Watching, Divna blinks with surprise. The snake seems as tame as a house cat. In a slow leisurely way he unfolds his sinuous length until he is lying flat against the ground, stretched out several feet long. He slithers toward the offering of baklava in Miranda's hand. She drops the pastry on the ground and smiles as the snake's tongue flashes out of his mouth and he swallows the sweet food.

Fascinated, Divna stares at the serpent disappearing in the tall grass at the side of the road. Her lips are slightly parted and she remains rapt, her hands on her hips.

Miranda stands up and stares at Divna with admiration. An impulse seizes her. She folds Divna in her arms and kisses her moist lips, lips that taste of brandy.

Releasing Divna suddenly, Miranda stands back and shakes her head in amazement. Her body still retains the impression of Divna's body, the feel of the other woman's large breasts against her own, and the newness of this pleases her and makes her laugh.

"I'm sorry. I didn't plan that. The impulse just came over me unexpectedly."

"That's okay. It happens sometimes. Nothing wrong with two women kissing, is there?"

"I guess not."

"Anyway, I'd better hurry. The children will be waking up."

Divna loops her arm around her new friend's waist and they continue walking toward the hotel.

They are approaching the long oval bend above the harbor where a high breakwater of gray stones rises, protecting the land from the often turbulent and dangerous tides. Beneath this barrier of stones the waves are pounding, hurling swirls of foam against the rocks where they crash, disintegrating into flocks of bubbles. The waves then recede, withdrawing quietly in large sweeping arcs of water that create scallops on the surface, before again gathering force and rushing forward to crash against the breakwater.

As they near the harbor, Miranda slows down, frowning. She makes Divna stop. "I thought I heard something—look!"

There is a black spot on the surface of the sea.

"What is it?"

"I think it's a person. Let's go!"

Miranda runs to the edge of the seawall, beckoning Divna to follow. The two women bend over the rocks, peering into the dark churning waters. Among the foam there appears for a second a black form, then a pale white shape. An arm breaks the surface, thrashes the air and disappears, sucked back into the sea.

With a single motion the women pull off their sandals and clamber over the wall, hurrying across the rocks to the sea. They fling themselves into the water, swimming toward the area where they saw the arm break the surface. A strong swimmer with an accurate eye, Miranda dives but does not see anything, dives again and still deeper until she catches sight of a pale white foot drifting up and down. Aiming for this foot, she dives, thrusting herself deep down in the water until she can seize it. She struggles to rise to the surface, but the drowning person is too heavy. The foot slips out of her hand. But she succeeds in grabbing hold of a mass of floating hair and strokes toward the surface. Paddling about the area of struggle, Divna remains nearer the safety of the shore. Grabbing Miranda's hand, Divna pulls her onto the rocks along with the person Miranda is towing.

Climbing back onto the road with their burden, the women find themselves staring at a naked boy with long hair. It's Rudy.

They pull him onto the rocks and turn him over so Miranda can kneel on his back and press the water from his lungs.

"Sh!" Miranda watches foam rush from the boy's mouth. She takes his wrist and feels his pulse. "He's still unconscious. But he's definitely alive."

"We'll have to carry him back to the hotel."

"We *have* to! But how?"

"I'll bend down. You lift him onto my shoulder. Then you stand up under his body so we can divide his weight between us."

"I don't think that will work." Divna frowns. "We'll have to make a swing with our hands."

"Okay. But we have to hurry."

"I know."

It is still early in the day. The air is soft and warm with little more than a hint of the hot dry heat to come.

The birds are singing with an air of nonchalance, and the cicadas have begun their rhythmic chirping at melodic intervals in the gathering brightness of the dawn.

Dionysios stands at the bow of the small boat, shielding his smarting eyes with one hand. As the boat rises and sinks back into the water, he finds himself yielding to the alternating motions of ascent and descent, submitting with pleasure to the swaying of the sea.

Shouting to his friend at the helm, Dionysios asks:

"It's pretty rough. Where can we put into port?"

"I'm not sure yet. Either Aghios Nicolaos or else Matalá."

"It doesn't matter." From either town he can catch a bus to Iraklion, luckily delaying his meeting with Divna for a few hours, giving himself a chance to prepare.

The rhythmic rising and falling of the boat with the waves takes on a reckless motion, an air of gaiety as they head toward the coast at Matalá, a strange rocky beach formed by an enormous wall of porous rock in which there are several hundred deep caves. As the distance between the boat and the harbor diminishes, Dionysios begins to hum some lines he recalls from his days at Oxford when, defying his father's wishes, he had studied both music and literature instead of law. The lines, which he cannot identify, possess a lulling sonority that tempts him to transform them into music.

When Divna opens the door of her hotel room, Bruno is standing beside the bed hurling his clothing into a suitcase. From the adjoining room come sounds of the children's murmurs and sniffles. Divna rushes past Bruno into the children's room. She finds Sasha in his pajamas curled up into a ball among rumpled sheets; the boy is rubbing his eyes and whimpering. Seated beside him, patting her brother's back with her small tanned hand, is Tamara.

Gathering the children into her arms, Divna comforts them with explanations of her absence:

"I only went for a walk. I couldn't sleep. You know, that happens to me a lot, and so I went for a walk." She holds the children tightly and strokes their heads, crooning as though they were still babies. Damn Bruno! He's a grown man, but he couldn't find a way to keep two children calm for two hours.

The door bursts open and Bruno stalks in, arms folded tightly across his chest. His face is twisted with anger. He demands:

"Where have you been?"

"Oh Bruno, I just went out for a walk. I couldn't sleep. I walked all the way to the Palace and back."

His expression conveys his certainty that she's lying.

"Bruno, darling, let's talk about it later." Divna is stripping off Sasha's pajamas and leading him toward the sink.

"Come on, children. Let's get ready for breakfast."

Smiling with relief, the boy and girl begin to wash and dress themselves. Tamara grins indulgently at her brother when he yells: "Mamma's back! Mamma's back! See, she came back! I told you she would!"

"Well, of course I came back."

Bruno is standing in the doorway between the two rooms with his arms still wrapped around his body in a challenging pose.

"Why is your dress soaked?"

Divna sighs. "Well, if you really have to know this very minute, I've been swimming."

"Swimming! You're nuts!"

"Naturally. Well, at the Palace there was another person who couldn't sleep."

"I just bet there was!"

"Oh calm down! It was a woman."

"Woman! Man! What difference does it make?"

With a shrug and half-smile, Divna replies: "Well, it makes a difference to *me*." Drying Sasha's face, she continues: "Anyway, the woman I accidentally met there is the dark one who was at the Dolphin Café last night."

"Oh *her*!"

"When we got nearly to the hotel, we heard a sound like a body hitting the water. And someone was drowning. A boy either fell or jumped into the sea."

Bruno glares at her. After a moment, while she helps the children choose shirts to wear with their shorts, he sneers:

"A boy fell into the sea. You must really think I'm a dope!"

There is a long pause before Divna murmurs: "Of course not."

"I am not a stupid man!" Bruno shouts. "Boys don't 'fall' into the sea!"

Above Sasha's head, Divna tries to signal caution, but it is too late; Tamara turns from the sink, her soapy face wrinkled, as she asks:

"Can children really *fall* into the sea?"

"It doesn't happen very often, Tamara. And then it happens only when they play on the rocks too close to the deep water. Don't worry, darling, it will never happen to either one of you because you are both good careful swimmers."

"Are you going to the dining room looking like that?" Bruno demands. He himself is smartly dressed in tight tan gabardine pants and a close-fitting Italian shirt the same shade of green as his eyes.

If he weren't so grouchy, Divna reflects, he would look like a young god. She glances at herself in the mirror and throws back her head, roaring with laughter. Her white dress is plastered to her body, outlining every lump of flesh, and her hair has begun to dry into a spongy mass of yellow frizz. Her eyes are red from lack of sleep and salt water. There is a long cut streaked with dried blood on her arm.

Once in the room she shares with Bruno, Divna allows herself a brief moment of self-defense.

"Honestly, I'm telling the truth! We saved a boy's life, that woman and I did. And you throw a stupid fit because you think I went out to meet a man in the middle of the night! Sometimes I just like to be alone for an hour or so. And look what happens! When I come back after an innocent walk, I find two scared kids who think they've been abandoned, and a man who's sure he's been crowned with horns!" Remembering Miranda's embrace, her innocent spontaneous kiss, Divna can't help grinning.

Reclining on the bed, folded arms behind his head, ankles crossed, Bruno watches Divna strip off her clammy dress. He stares at her body with a ravenous yet resentful look, as though he yearns to feel superior to the attraction that keeps him with this woman he can't intimidate.

Observing his face in the mirror above the bureau, Divna remarks:

"You're looking at me the way a fat man looks at a freshly baked pizza."

"Oh shut up!" Bruno growls. "Is it really true about the boy you say you saved?"

Divna is bending over, drying her body with a towel. "Of course it's true!"

There are three dresses hanging in her closet; all three are white. Divna takes a fresh one with a full skirt, tying it at her waist with a belt of purple and orange embroidery and long woolen flounces. She rubs her face clean with a wad of cotton, paints her lashes with mascara, coats her lips with a colorless gloss, and runs her hands through her hair to fluff it up.

"Let's go. I'm starving!"

"I really think I should be fed up with you," Bruno proclaims, languidly rising from the bed with a melodramatic shake of his slender torso.

Turning to face him squarely, hands on hips, Divna states in a level emotionless tone:

"If you think you *should*, darling Bruno, then you should." With that, she walks toward the door and opens it. "Come on, Bruno! The kids and I are hungry. You can decide whether you're going to leave me after you've had breakfast."

Suddenly, Bruno starts hooting. "Divna, you're such an ass! You forgot to put on your shoes!"

Miranda is sitting in the waiting room of Iraklion's hospital. Rudy hasn't yet regained consciousness. The hospital is in the center of the town on a crowded narrow street, and the waiting room is buried in the center of the hospital. It has no windows.

She fans her face with a magazine. On the cover is a photo of the Pope denouncing feminist theology and the "demonic" idolatry of goddess worship. This makes her smile. Overhead a huge electric fan squeaks as it turns.

The door of the waiting room opens and the doctor comes in. He is a young man who speaks nearly perfect English. His manner is dejected, fatigued as though only a few years of battling disease have permanently soured his disposition. He takes off his glasses, rubbing a deep ridge across his nose.

"How well do you know this boy?"

"I don't know him at all. I've seen him at the hotel pool. And yesterday we ran into each other at Knossos and we talked. That's all."

"Do you think he jumped?"

"I have no idea. He might have slipped. Maybe he was drunk."

"Do you mind if I ask what you were doing on that deserted road at dawn?"

Miranda raises her chin. She feels pugnacious, resentful of the doctor's nosiness. "You may not believe me, but I had insomnia. Someone in my hotel was playing some awful music over and over again. So I thought a long walk would help me relax. I've walked to Knossos alone at night several times. It seems safe."

"Yes, it's safe enough. And the other woman? Was she suffering from insomnia too?"

"No, something else. A fight with her boyfriend, I think. That was it. I don't know her."

"We know her. Her husband is a Greek. A very well known composer and singer."

He knows the husband, so he thinks he knows her, Miranda notes. In a calm tone, she inquires about Rudy's condition.

With a severe, almost contemptuous look, he replies, "Listen, he's only a kid. Yet he's traveling all by himself in a foreign country. What kind of parents allow that! He has a concussion. Who was he with when you last saw him?"

"Some Greek boys he met at a pastry shop. Maybe they were drinking."

The doctor sighs and nods. "In any case you and Maljković saved his life."

"I guess we did. But I don't really know this boy," Miranda insists.

"Well, you may *have* to know him. At least for a while. He's a kid, like I said. I think he tried to kill himself. You people don't seem to understand that—you and Maljković." The doctor looks around, as though Divna were in the room with them. "But you did a good job. Who performed the artificial respiration?"

"I did."

"Good. How long are you going to stay here on Crete?"

"A while. I'm not sure exactly how long."

"Come back tomorrow. Rudy will want to see you both when he's conscious again and has rested."

In a hotel room at Matalá, Dionysios stands in front of a mirror combing his slightly long black hair to one side and squinting into his reddened eyes. A fine meal and a half liter of retsina have restored his mood of confidence. A survey of his face in the mirror reassures him that his period of hiding out hasn't wrecked his looks as badly as he'd thought. He seems tired but far from ravaged. Divna may never even notice his injured hand. He pats cologne on his cheeks.

Taking a pack of cigarettes and a handkerchief from his bag, he looks himself over again and leaves. He feels proud of himself for having dismissed the vengeful fantasy that Divna will look worn and strained from working too hard.

In the lobby of the hotel is a small bar. Dionysios stops and quickly downs a glass of ouzo. It will warm him, help him feel less resentful, less angry, friendlier toward Divna and more relaxed with his children.

There are several men clustered around the bar gossiping about two very large women who dove into the sea to rescue a drowning boy. The storyteller says that one of the women was fair and the other dark. He says that the women were naked and that after they pulled the boy out of the sea, they carried him to the hospital. He says that he actually saw these women. He claims they were tall, strong, beautiful, with full lush bodies like the goddesses of the antique days.

Dionysios smiles and downs a second glass of ouzo. When it comes to women there is nothing to compare with the credulousness of his countrymen. If women are involved, these men are always ready to believe in miracles.

Just before noon, the island is assaulted by a strong summer storm. Hot winds churn and whip the waves, battering and slamming them against the breakwater. Dark gray clouds cluster just above the sea, with the ominous smokiness of a fire smothered by a damp blanket. A steady threat of suffocation weights the air with menace.

In the dining room of the hotel a waiter stands beside a table occupied by a family of four. He waits, with a pad in his hand, a pencil raised above it.

"Mamma, I'm so hungry!"

Tamara and Sasha lean closer to their mother, who is scanning the menu with a worried expression, her forehead bisected by a vertical frown.

Bruno sits with his chin cupped in his palm, his other hand punctuating the air with impatience. "But why do you want to see that kid? I don't understand."

"Let's talk about it later. Sasha, please take your fingers out of your mouth. You're going to eat in a few minutes."

"I want shishkebab. Mamma, can I have whatever I want to eat?"

"But *why* do you have to see him?"

"Bruno, are you ready to order? The waiter is *waiting*." Divna rubs the back of her neck, frowns.

With a look of scarcely veiled contempt, the waiter addresses Bruno: "*Sir?*"

"Okay! Okay, I'm ready. One shishkebab. A cheese and spinach pie. One order of red snapper. Moussaka. Four salads and another liter of Domestica."

"Thank you, sir," snaps the waiter, stalking toward the kitchen.

"Mamma, when is Daddy coming to get us?"

"Today. Some time later today. Don't worry, darling. He'll be here soon. I'm sure he will." Sighing, Divna wipes her perspiring forehead with the back of her hand. She rummages through her handbag, searching for a tissue. She pulls the collection of Strindberg plays out of her bag and tosses it onto an empty chair.

"Can you tell me, please, why you want to see that kid?" Bruno's face is contorted with frustration and jealousy. "Don't you realize there's been some kind of crime? There's going to be an ugly mess. Divna, you're going to be in the middle of a Greek scandal."

"A Greek scandal! That's very funny, Bruno. My marriage is as hot a Greek scandal as I can stand. Thanks. Let's talk about it later."

"Why can't we talk about it now?"

"Mamma, Mamma, when's my shishkebab coming? I'm so hungry!"

"In a minute, darling. Please try to sit still. You're kicking my leg."

Just as Divna raises her wine glass to her lips, Sasha lurches across the table and accidentally bumps her arm. Red wine splashes over the front of her white dress. Wiping at the wine with a napkin, Divna silently makes a decision: Bruno is leaving sooner than he thinks.

Unfolding her napkin, Tamara gets up and scurries around the table to her mother, carefully tucking the serviette into the neck of Divna's dress. "Poor little Mamma!"

"Poor little Mamma! Always a mess!" Divna quickly hugs her

daughter and pats her shoulder as a gesture of gratitude for the child's tenderness.

The waiter approaches with a tray loaded with succulent-smelling food.

"There's really no reason for you to see him," Bruno continues. "You'll just get involved." He pours a second glass of wine for Divna, then shakes his head slowly: "I don't understand you."

"I guess not," she agrees, raising a fork loaded with cheese and spinach pie to her lips.

Closing the drapes and stripping off her clothes, Miranda lies down and tries to nap. But she's too tense. Turning over, she buries her face in the pillow as she used to do when she was a young girl suffering terrible seizures of menstrual pain. But even the remembrance of a physical comfort as elementary as a heating pad on a cramping abdomen fails to bring relief. She feels overwhelmed by anguish and anxiety, anxiety caused partly by the dramatic events of the last few hours and partly by her shame at having clasped Divna in a sensual embrace. Miranda knows that if Divna were to assure her that it was a meaningless or at least a harmless action, she would soon regain her equanimity. Never before has she been conscious of the appeal of a woman's body. Even today when the impulse seized her, it wasn't something she could have denied even if she had reflected on the consequences of her action before committing it. She senses that there is a power, a latent power deep within her body that she has never allowed herself to experience. So when it came so suddenly, she was totally overwhelmed by the spontaneous force of her ardor.

Reaching for the telephone, she asks for Divna's room.

The voice that responds is filled with a taut sense of expectation. Could Divna have been expecting her call?

"Divna, I'd like to talk to you about what happened this morning. Do you have a few minutes? Maybe some time later this afternoon?"

The answer is a puzzled-sounding echo ending with a question: "What happened this morning? Oh, you mean that boy! Yes, we should do something about him. Go to see him. I want to visit him."

"Oh, definitely! I went to the hospital this morning but he was still unconscious. No, what I meant was something else." Miranda waits.

The response is a burst of merry laughter. "Oh that! But what is there to talk about? It was a natural thing. A beautiful thing."

"Do you really think so?"

"Of course! Listen, Miranda, are you looking out the window right now? The storm has cleared. The sun is shining. Shall we meet on the beach, say, at about three? We can talk more then."

Such casualness astounds Miranda, who can't help wishing she herself were free enough even to envy Divna's naturalness. In a sense, Miranda feels that she has been rebuked subtly, rebuked for putting her own neurotic anxiety before the welfare of that sad boy. Divna-the-Good has released her from her guilt and, therefore, has freed Miranda to focus on a question that is almost as urgent and as interesting as her own sexuality— whether she ought to remain on Crete a while longer or return to Korchula and try to paint again. But if, when she sails back to her tiny house and to her rocky perch above the sea, to her painting and—above all—to her solitude, if then she's still unable to paint, she will have to go back to New York City where her former—safe—life is waiting for her.

On a table beside Miranda's bed rests a magnificent shell, the one Marinos gave her, a Conch of Venus whose formal name "Ovula ovum Linne" tells as much as its informal one does about its association with woman's body. The Ovula is formed like a smooth glossy fine-grained pear nestling inside a hood of gleaming white porcelain. Between the inward-curving surfaces of the Ovula, coiling in upon itself, and the elongated sweep of the scalloped fold of the shell, there lies deep inside the beautiful form an absolutely impenetrable darkness—a darkness of surprising density whose impermeability is intensified by the fragile glowing white of the shell's outer surface.

Consoled, Miranda sits on the edge of her bed for a while holding the Ovula, stroking its curves and crying quietly.

Eventually, the heroic Ovula brings a sense of calm. She will have to confront her inner turbulence; that's obvious. But she feels helpless to do that without forgetting, dismissing once and for all time, the stranger who had loved her with such tender passion before disappearing while she lay asleep on the rocks above the sea.

The beach at the hotel is a crescent splay of sand speckled with red, blue and yellow umbrellas under which small groups of people roost like birds at their baths, sprinkling their feathers with water, shaking their wings, preening in the shallow waters of a fountain where they can—if they are tempted—stare at their own rippled reflections.

In a tight black bathing suit that controls her abundant curves and lights up her blonde curls with its contrasting density, Divna sits on a beach chair with her legs crossed just as though she were at home watching television. She drinks Coca Cola from a can.

At her feet lies Bruno, resting on one elbow. He is wearing brief shiny-textured foam green trunks that tightly cup his ample sex organs. He, too, sips a Coke as he flips through the pages of an Italian scandal sheet.

Squatting at the water's edge, Tamara and Sasha are patting and shaping mounds of wet sand into a castle. They play with the intense concentration of scientists working on a research project. But Sasha seems uneasy. From time to time he glances at his mother to reassure himself that she's still here while Tamara, on the other hand, appears calm and self-possessed. Like Divna, Tamara has adopted a mask of casualness, as if she has already learned that the only security possible is the certainty of being able to depend on herself. Sometimes when Sasha glances at Divna, his face grows tense with apprehension, but after he gains control of this emotion, he once again allows his features to portray devotion.

With a supple grace that disappoints none of his admirers,

Bruno languidly gets up and announces:

"I'm going now."

Glancing at her watch, Divna comments: "Dionysios is late."

"I don't think you heard what I said. I'm fed up. I'm leaving. For good."

Divna's response is a light laugh and a wave of her hand. "It had to happen. Sooner or later." As she watches Bruno slink back toward the hotel, she thinks about her husband, the man she will soon meet to talk about the details of divorce, and wonders why she feels so uneasy. She does not love Dionysios any more than she hates him, even though there was a time when his slightest touch aroused instant desire. But that was long ago.

Yawning, Divna glances around the beach at the varied tourists: the rich kids from the States, the middle-aged couples from Scandinavia, Germany and Holland, turning bright pink in the underwear they insist on wearing to sunbathe, the flocks of Greek children scampering up and down the beach trying to sell dark glasses, suntan lotion and European newspapers.

She waves at Miranda who is approaching wearing a purple and white striped bathing suit and a gold scarf. Under her arm is a large book, *The Nature of Space*, by someone named Irene Rice Pereira. Much as Divna likes Miranda, she also pities her a little because of her shyness and the way she seems to worry so much about what's "normal."

"Hi! Sit down here. Have you rested up?"

A shrill cry. Tamara has shoved Sasha into the sand castle, crushing it. Both the children are yelling and shoving. Divna waits to see whether intervention is necessary.

Addressing Miranda, she exclaims, "Children!—you're lucky not to have any—at least not yet. They eat, sleep, drink, hate, love, fight, kiss, nothing at all profound!" Secretly Divna wishes that she could love both her children with the same degree of fervent intensity. But the mother who loves all her children impartially hasn't yet been born, she assures herself.

"When I was young, Miranda, we girls often kissed and embraced each other."

"Did you? I guess we just didn't have the nerve where I grew up."

Divna shrugs. "Well, you know, we did that before we discovered the men."

"Oh yes! The men."

Miranda's bitter tone makes Divna laugh. "Listen, Miranda, I have to take the kids up and put them down for naps. I'll come right back and we'll have a swim. Okay?"

Ten minutes later Miranda is soaring out over the sea in a swing. The midday storm has left behind a clear deep blue sky scored with stark white clouds.

Flying through the air, Miranda pumps as she propels herself over the water, arching backward so that her hair streams behind her as she flies.

She lets go of the swing and dives into the water where she paddles around a while before turning onto her back. Now Divna runs into the water and turns quickly onto her back, floating beside Miranda. Their heads glide through the water side by side.

"Your guy Bruno is very attractive."

"Yes, I guess so. He's gone. He got fed up. Men never stay with me."

"Men don't stay with you! That's hard to believe!"

"It's true, all the same. They like to try to conquer me. I think that's the attraction. They want to see if they can do it.

But I'm too independent. Sooner or later, they get fed up and just leave."

"They leave me too. I'm not sure why. I don't understand myself as well as you seem to know yourself. A man just abandoned me. That's partly why I'm here."

"Because of some *man!*"

"Partly. What happened was that when he left, I was so upset I couldn't paint any more."

"Oh well, that's different. Did you love him?"

"I don't know. I just don't know. Divna, I'm not even sure who he is."

"What? How could you not be sure who he is?"

"Well, I met him on the island of Korchula in the Adriatic Sea. I thought he was a Croatian peasant."

Divna stands up and starts walking toward the shore.

Miranda follows.

"Croatian peasant, you say. I know the type. My husband's mother has a house on Korchula. And I've spent some time there. *Ludi Boja!* That's absolutely the worst kind of man! They're awful!"

"Well, it turns out he wasn't Croatian after all; he was a Greek. And he was very sweet, until he left me."

"Still, it must be terrible—not to want to paint any more."

"*Terrible!* I feel dead. As soon as I find out Rudy's going to be okay, that he has enough money to get home and things like that, I'm going back to Korchula."

"To get back with that man! I think that's a little—well, pardon me, Miranda—but that's not very smart."

"No, really, I'm going back to try to paint. But if I still have this block, I'll just have to give up and go back to New York."

Their conversation is interrupted by a thump and a splash.

A blond man has hurled himself into the water, causing waves to rise around their ankles. He has a big red ball tucked under one arm. He throws the ball to Miranda, and as she reaches up, she notices that his eyes are making a leisurely tour of her body.

She tosses the ball to Divna, who flings herself back into the waves and swims toward it.

While Miranda watches, the stranger swims after Divna, who rises out of the water and hurls the ball to Miranda. She is waiting, laughing, hands in the air.

As he walks through the dining room of the hotel to the beach where, he has been told, his wife is relaxing, Dionysios Marinos Costeletos pauses to watch two women and a man who are playing ball near the shore. It is several seconds before he absorbs the fact that one of the women is the artist he walked away from several weeks earlier on Korchula. This unpleasant, or maybe pleasant discovery, he isn't sure which, is magnified by another. The other woman is his wife.

M ore than an hour later, Dionysios is finally able to approach Divna. She is drying off in a beach chair, drinking a Coke, lying back with her eyes closed. She seems to have forgotten their appointment.

"Divna, I'm here. I'm sorry I'm late."

Opening her eyes slowly, Divna smiles at the man who's standing in front of her, his expression serious, even apprehensive.

"That's all right. How could you expect to be on time, under the circumstances? Shall we go in? The children are taking their naps."

Everyone on the beach watches the couple, their curiosity aroused by the disappearance of one man an hour or so earlier, and now the appearance of another one.

"Divna, why are they staring?"

"Why are you asking me? You're a Greek. You should know that they always stare a lot. Shall we go inside?"

At first the two children stare at Dionysios, uncertain whether to come to greet him. At a signal from Divna, however, they scramble off their beds and rush toward their father. Tamara leans against his leg, taking his hand and rubbing it against her cheek. But Sasha, after an initial outburst of happiness, withdraws a little, waiting, watching with curious and suspicious eyes.

"Mamma made Bruno mad, so he went away," Tamara explains, beaming at her father.

"So this time it was a Bruno," Dionysios remarks, aiming the comment at his wife's back.

"Last night when Mamma was gone so long, Bruno was crabby." Tamara adds her opinion that "Bruno was a grouch and so when Mamma came back all wet, he was mean to her."

Smiling faintly, Dionysios just nods. "How are you, Divna."

"Oh, a little sad." She takes off her dark glasses and gazes at Dionysios with frank affection. "Aren't you sad?"

"Yes I am." He adds, "It's not being in love any longer."

Walking to the window, looking at the sea, Divna corrects: "I didn't say I wasn't in love. I never said that."

"You're in love with Bruno then." But he's teasing.

"And you? You must be in love with someone else too."

"No, I'm not."

"No, I don't think so. But you're definitely not in love with me."

"Not with anyone else either."

"I hope not. I'm selfish about that. I still care about you."

"I care about you too."

"But we can't get along together."

"Absolutely not."

"This is a stupid conversation."

There is a long silence during which Divna watches a motor launch speed across the horizon. She still isn't totally immune to Dionysios's physical presence; for one thing, his body always seems to generate waves of heat. It's doing that now.

"Where are you planning to take the children?"

"First to Athens and then to Korchula."

Tamara jumps up dancing. "We're going away with Daddy! We're going away with Daddy!"

"I'm not going!" Sasha yells.

Running her hand through his hair, Divna promises: "You'll

have lots of fun. There's a donkey you can ride. And a pretty dog."

The boy pouts but stops complaining.

Tamara throws herself on her stomach on her mother's bed, cups her chin in her hands and gazes at her father:

"You're not pretty," she proclaims, "but you're nice."

"Who'll be with you on Korchula?"

"Just Mother." With a short laugh, Dionysios asks: "Have you heard, Esma's talking about getting married?"

"Married! Your *mother* is talking about getting married!"

"Well, she's never *been* married."

They laugh.

"Oh, I'm *so* sorry we get along so badly! You can be so much fun!" Divna's tone is merry but her eyes are glistening.

"I *was* fun maybe, not any more. I'm worn out. I haven't recovered yet."

"You look just fine. Better than before. More mature."

Changing the subject, Dionysios teases: "And where *were* you last night? Being unfaithful to the great god Bruno?" In the past it had often been good strategy to put Divna on the defensive; rooted in instinctive directness, she usually didn't suspect that she was being manipulated. He's surprised at how much pleasure there is—still—in teasing her.

"Where I was last night can't be any of *your* business." She chuckles, vowing to get Dionysios into bed before the night ends.

Sasha has fallen asleep lying on the bed beside his sister. Tamara goes on staring at her father with radiant fascination.

"Why can't you live with us, Daddy?"

"Shut up!" Divna orders in a level tone. "You don't know anything about grown-ups."

"You're silly," Tamara retorts.

"I see Tamara has inherited your self-control."

"Don't be sarcastic." Turning quickly, Divna exclaims: "Last night! What a story! You should have seen Bruno's face when I came in at dawn with my dress soaking wet and my hair frizzed up!"

"What were you doing? Water skiing?"

"I was helping rescue a drowning boy."

Dionysios recalls the story he heard earlier in the day about two heroic women pulling a boy out of the sea.

"I heard something about that. Who was the other woman?"

"An American. A painter who's here on vacation. Why? Do you know her?"

"Why should I know her? And what if I do? You and I aren't—"

"I know. I know."

"Yes you are married! You still are married!" Tamara screeches.

"We might be married," Divna asserts, "but we don't live together any more, and we aren't going to. Tamara, don't try to tell grown-ups what to do." Ignoring Tamara's answering grimace, Divna turns back to Dionysios and asks: "Now, about Miranda—"

"I think she might be the same woman who had a little one-room house on Korchula. That's all."

"You had an affair with her."

"Well, not exactly. But she probably thought I wanted to, something like that," Dionysios concedes, with a warning look at Tamara, who is standing by the bed, frowning.

"Tamara, go to your room and put on a dress to wear to dinner." Raising her arms, Divna fluffs her hair around her face. "Well, why *didn't* you have an affair with her? She's very attractive. Nice too."

"You didn't finish telling me about the boy you two rescued."

"You didn't finish telling me about Miranda on Korchula."

Dionysios drops onto the bed beside Sasha. "There's nothing to tell. She came there to paint. Her father died, left her a little money. She works hard as a teacher. So she came away to paint. She didn't know anyone. She was painting. That's all."

"She's a very good-looking woman. And a fine swimmer."

"Uh huh." Dionysios begins to rub his wrist. "I felt sorry for her. As I said, she didn't know anyone. So I took her some gifts."

"I bet you did." Divna strikes a pose, bending slightly backward, hands on her hips. "I bet she enjoyed them too."

"Divna, you're being ridiculous!"

"What did you take her?"

"Well, I pretended to be a peasant. A local oaf. So I took her things like—oh—cheese. *Prosciut*. A loaf of bread. Rose petal brandy. Flowers. Things like that."

"And then?"

"Well, then I really began to take her paintings seriously. You know me."

"Oh yes I do."

"Well, she's a really good artist. Her paintings are original. And powerful."

"She must have been happy to have an admirer of her paintings. Especially in such a lonely place as Korchula."

"Well yes, I think she was. But then she didn't know what to make of me. She thought I was a fisherman. Or a stone-cutter. It was confusing to her, because I seemed to have insights into her paintings that she didn't expect from a—a primitive."

Divna runs her hand through her curls. "But you didn't seduce her?"

"Oh no. Of course, I didn't seduce her."

"Hmm.... You must have changed. But none of this is my business."

"You're right. It isn't."

"Let's meet for dinner later at the Dolphin Café, at the harbor."

"Why that one? There are better restaurants."

Divna flings her hands in the air and throws back her head, laughing. "It's just the way it used to be—being with you. All right then, you choose the restaurant. We'll meet wherever you want."

"The Dolphin is all right." But Dionysios is suspicious. Divna has an irresponsible sense of humor. He suspects that she's already arranged for Miranda to go to the Dolphin Café too. Still, he agrees.

Mimicking a pout, Divna becomes conciliatory. "You really don't want to go to that one, do you? Okay then. Choose another place."

He snaps: "Look, I'm tired. I spent the night in a small boat. It was damp and cold. I didn't sleep. I need to rest before dinner."

"Why do we always fight?"

"Because you're crazy."

"You're perverse. Whatever I say, you say the opposite."

"The Dolphin at seven-thirty. Goodbye."

Dionysios doesn't slam the door but closes it decisively to express his impatience. This meeting has already become difficult in exactly the way he'd hoped it wouldn't, and he wonders whether Miranda's coincidental presence may not turn out to be helpful in establishing a more or less amiable distance between Divna and himself. She continues to amaze but no longer to amuse him; definitely, he isn't in love with her any more. As he hurries down the corridor outside her room, Dionysios hears Divna's laughter, a bit unnatural, almost pained. And now, against his will, he is touched, remembering her considerable skill at masking her disappointments, even her rare moods of despondency.

Divna hurls herself on the bed beside Sasha and lies staring up at the ceiling. If she isn't careful to control her feelings, she'll cry in front of Sasha. And if she cries, she'll make her eyes red and puffy. Now she regrets having let Bruno go off; if he were still with her, she'd at least have an escort, someone to go out with her in public.

She sits up, raises her arms and jerks off her wrinkled beach robe. She throws it on the floor, flops down again, this time on her stomach, and begins to cry.

But after the first few stinging tears, she stops weeping. She can't afford to look terrible for the rest of the evening. Worst of all, Dionysios would have the satisfaction of knowing he still has the power to make her cry! She folds a wet handkerchief into a compress and rests with the cloth over her eyes.

How she'd love to throw her arms around Aunt Mileva right now! What a wise old woman! She'd warned Divna that it was stupid to marry a Greek!

/\s she begins to change for the evening, Miranda considers inviting Divna to go to dinner with her. After all, Divna's alone now too. The maid shared with Miranda the staff's gossip about the details of Bruno's leaving, stalking off the beach like a sulking prince. But when Miranda rings Divna's room, one of the children tells her that Divna's sleeping and has left instructions not to be disturbed.

Sketchbook sticking out of her burlap shoulder bag, Miranda sets off for the center of town. Her first stop is the hospital to see whether Rudy's regained consciousness. A nurse tells her that he's much better; in fact, he's expected to recover with relatively little damage to his nervous system. But it's still too soon for him to have visitors.

Extremely relieved, her mood much lighter, Miranda strolls along the breakwater, hoping that Divna and the children will come to the Dolphin Café later.

Dionysios is swinging around the bend of the harbor, feeling apprehensive but better physically than he has in many days, when he catches sight, a few yards ahead, of the woman he wants to avoid. She has paused beside the sea wall to make some quick sketches. He admires her outfit, a black skirt with a Greek key emblem decorating the border and a dark red peasant blouse. Over her arm is a shawl woven in many shades of gold, brown and scarlet.

From the beginning when he first saw this woman on the island of Korchula, Dionysios was attracted by the simple, apparently brave way she accepted, or even embraced her self-chosen solitude. She seems to have the gift of steady inward-directed attentiveness, and even though she isn't a beautiful woman, she arouses in him an urgent desire, compelling him to face again the passions that in the past have brought acute disappointment, even suffering. And yet when he looks at Miranda and balances his fears against his attraction, he decides to try to talk to her.

He walks to the breakwater and pauses, leaning against it and pretending to be absorbed by the grayish violet evening sea.

Miranda stands sketching, at the same time enjoying the smells of roasting lamb and vegetables that drift toward the harbor from Iraklion's many outdoor tavernas. When she notices Dionysios, at first she doesn't recognize him and dismisses him as just another island male trying to pick up a tourist.

Without looking at her, he begins to sing the most seductive song in his repertoire, "The Bedouin Love Song."

"I would rather you hit me with the edge of a sword than have you look at me with sad eyes...."

But she just glides away from him, moving quickly. He admires her long straight back, the carriage made straighter by her anger. Raising his voice, Dionysios sings louder.

"....rather than have you look at me with sad eyes...."

Miranda begins to run, holding her bag steady with one hand, dark hair flying behind her. When he overtakes her, she's muttering dire threats against Greek men.

An elderly man comes out of a tourist shop and watches, clearly amused.

Dionysios goes on singing "The Bedouin Love Song" in spite of Miranda's resistance.

"Is this love—you won't even say farewell to me...."

Glaring, she orders: "Leave me alone. I am *not* going to say please."

Shrugging, still singing, he walks at her side.

"Do you find joy in the evil things that have happened to me...."

Finally, his song having ended, Dionysios remarks: "You are amazingly rude."

Miranda stops suddenly and glares at him. "You fraud," she hisses. "What sort of game were you playing with me?" She stalks ahead, swinging her bag angrily. "As far as I'm concerned, we have *not* met, and I don't *want* to meet you now."

"Maybe not, but fortunately or unfortunately, depending on a person's point of view, we *have* met." He gives her a playful look.

"Well then, we're never going to meet again."

He risks lightly touching her arm. "You don't look so nice when you're mad."

A passing couple stops, arms linked, heads together, watching what promises to be a good scene.

"Leave me alone!" Miranda hisses.

Smiling, staring at her profile, Dionysios teases her: "So we have not met. I'm the man you met on the island of Korchula. I'm the man who visited you by boat. I'm the man who brought you gifts. I'm the man who...."

"Shut up! People are staring at us!"

"Greeks love scenes. They'll think we're married."

Hurling him a look of fury, she snaps: "Your singing voice is foul."

He shrugs and grins. "Nobody likes it—at first." He begins a reprise of "The Bedouin Love Song."

"I would rather you hit me with the edge of a sword...."

Rearing back like a horse ready to pitch an offensive rider into the dirt, Miranda swings her bag at him. "Stop singing that damned song!"

"You're the nastiest woman I've ever known!"

"You're the meanest man!"

"Mean! What do you mean, *mean*?"

"Leaving me alone on Korchula."

"That was bad. I admit. Oh Miranda, I'm sorry. I can explain it. I really can. I didn't want to hurt you. It was something I couldn't help doing."

"Hurt me! What in the world makes you think you *hurt* me?"

"Look, can we talk about this later tonight? Please, let me at least try to explain why I disappeared the way I did."

"No." Head in the air, Miranda continues toward her destination, the Dolphin Café. "I'm leaving tomorrow."

"You're leaving? Where're you going?"

"Back to New York. I'm going back to New York, and I'm probably going to stay there."

"Where men are never 'mean' to women?"

"You and I will never see each other again."

"Maybe not. So isn't that a good reason to listen to what I have to say about why I left Korchula?"

"No."

"Well, you're obviously very angry. But I like you just as much as before."

"Thanks. But I don't like you at all." She hurls him a look intended to be hateful.

"I guess you don't. What time are you leaving tomorrow?"

"In the morning. Early."

"Well then, since we're never going to meet again, I should introduce myself."

"Isn't your name Marinos? That's what you told me."

"That's the name my stepmother gave me. But that's not my real name. And she's not my real mother."

"What difference does it make to me?"

"To you, none maybe. But to me my name makes a lot of difference."

"All right, what's your 'real' name?"

"Dionysios."

She laughs, scoffing. "Am I really supposed to believe that!"

"Well, sure. It's not such a stupid name."

"I didn't mean to suggest that it's stupid. It's just— different."

"I can't imagine why I like you so much! I must be crazy!"

Silence.

Then, "Well, I really don't *want* you to like me."

"You're having some success at that. Believe me. Listen, Miranda. Please let me talk to you."

They are standing in front of the Dolphin Café. Red and blue lights swing across the façade in loops of bright color. From inside comes noise, activity, music. Inside, people are having fun. Miranda puts her hand on the door.

Just as she is about to step inside the café, Dionysios puts his hand on her arm, promising, "Some day I'll sing that song to you again. And some day you'll hear its beauty, even in my rasping voice."

Whirling, she snaps, "Beauty! Do you know what hurt me the most! You did something terrible to me! I can't paint any more!" Flouncing about, Miranda stalks across the threshold into the restaurant. Her eyes search the faces at the tables. She waits, paralyzed with fury.

The music is loud and boisterous, gay, vivid, with shrill clarinets and jangling tambourines that punctuate the beats of several drums. People are dancing, with Divna in the lead, hands on her hips, at the head of a chain of men, women and children who are winding a narrow path through the restaurant, a serpentine coil of energetically moving figures. Behind Divna is Sasha, tightly clutching his mother's waist, and behind him, Tamara, swaying from side to side as she moves, eyes closed; and so the chain of dancers continues to sweep and sway in and around the tables, moving to the music that fills the bright room.

Divna looks at the doorway, noticing Miranda standing alone in the dusk, and just outside, Dionysios. He seems uncertain whether to come inside. Divna stares at them for several seconds.

Among the musicians on a small raised dais is the same woman as on the previous night, a plump dark woman with wildly curling black hair falling over her shoulders and tumbling down her back, a woman dressed in many skirts and blouses, all jingling with gold coins. And lying against her forehead, like the fringe of her cap of gold, are still more glittering coins.

A tambourine in one hand, head thrown back in an attitude of abandonment, the woman sings wildly, her song piercing the air with passion. Transfixed, Miranda remains inside the doorway, staring at this woman who has no fear of giving herself totally to her emotions.

Dionysios pushes his way past her through the spiraling dancers until he reaches the platform where the gypsy singer stands. When she sees him, the woman hurls her tambourine into the air and flings her arms around him with such force that she nearly throws them both off the small platform. Dionysios wraps the woman in his arms and hugs her tightly for all to see.

Miranda stares, amazed and furious, torn between a desire to hurry back to the her room in the hotel, where humiliating incidents can no longer harm her, and an equally strong desire to stay, if only to see what will happen next. She is joined by Divna, who shakes her arm slightly and inclines her head, as if to share a secret. When Miranda reluctantly looks up, returning the other woman's gaze, she finds to her surprise, that Divna's eyes are moist.

"That's his mother," Divna explains with an air of satisfaction. "He didn't know she was here. I arranged their meeting as a surprise."

"His *mother*!" Miranda echoes. "She seems too young!"

For a moment, Divna stares at Miranda, as if surprised by her naïveté. "She's not from a 'civilized' country like you. She's a gypsy. Gypsy girls are sold to their husbands when they're ten or eleven years old. Esma was only twelve when Dionysios was born."

Nodding, Miranda feels herself grow warm with a new and previously unsuspected insight. "Do you know him very well? You seem to know a lot about him."

"Sooner or later, someone will tell you. We used to be married. But not any longer. It's over now." But Divna doesn't get to finish the consoling explanation she'd planned for Miranda. The other woman shakes off her hand and streaks out of the restaurant, once again fleeing alone into the night.

Dionysios closes the door of his wife's room and steps into the corridor of the hotel. Divna, the crafty peasant, has gotten him into bed against his will. He feels exhausted and disgusted with himself for yielding. So worn out he wants to fall on his face, he leaves the hotel. His enthusiasm for love has been shattered by too many disappointments. He is too dispirited to pursue Miranda right now.

At least at this particular moment. He needs to rest first.

Divna tiptoes to the door of the children's room and opens it a crack. Sasha is sound asleep, sprawled on his stomach with his arms flung above his head. However, Tamara is lying on her back gazing at the ceiling with wide dreamy eyes. The child is humming softly, holding her interlaced fingers together on her breast. At the sight of her mother, Tamara raises one finger to her lips, warning her not to disturb Sasha.

Nodding with amusement, Divna softly closes the door. She has work to do. Her three dresses are all dirty. And there's a scene in "Hippolytus" that needs work, for the role of Phaedra suits her temperament well in some respects but not so well in others, and she's still having difficulty achieving credibility in her accusation of Hippolytus. She doesn't want to give a bad performance here in Greece where success in the classical repertoire carries the greatest professional significance.

Filling the small sink with water, she stuffs in her dresses and rubs them with the scrap of spicy-scented soap that Bruno left behind. It's good to be alone again, she notes, as she scrubs a wine stain on her white dress. And, yes, she tells herself, she was right to test Dionysios's feelings by luring him into bed. Humming as she scrubs, she feels a luxurious drowsiness begin to seep through her body, starting with her toes. A languor rises through her legs and stomach, a weariness as pleasant and persuasive as a glass of wine.

Luring Dionysios into bed probably wasn't a smart idea, but having done it, she feels a sense of triumph over him. Maybe it's only a temporary triumph, but right now it feels satisfying.

With a noisy yawn, Divna lets the water run out of the sink and begins to squeeze the soap out of her dresses.

In the morning she will go visit the boy in the hospital.

Having spent most of the evening packing, Miranda finds, to her surprise, that she is very sleepy and quite relaxed, maybe because of her decision to leave Crete tomorrow on the noon boat.

Toward midnight, however, she is awakened by a light tapping at the door. Putting her ear to the door, she hears rustling sounds. Then more light tapping.

"Who's there?" she whispers as loudly as possible.

"Miranda, please! Please let me in so I can talk to you!" It's the man who calls himself Marinos, or Dionysios, or whatever.

For a moment she tries to imagine what would happen if she were to admit this treacherous stranger. The result is a vision of a banal scene replayed in her imagination from a dozen or so past conflicts with men. The intruder will apologize for his insensitivity and cruelty, and then with the arrogance of a successful suppliant, he will try to make love to her, fully assured of her ardent—perhaps urgent—need of his caresses. Then, after a reluctant reconciliation, should she be foolish enough to let it take place, the same old routine of petty dishonesty and small betrayals will start all over again, and she will be left hanging, yes, again, from the rack of a rawly-scored love.

After a while, the man on the other side of the door begins to whisper her name in a hoarse, ragged tone. But she's no fool,

Miranda tells herself. She knows he doesn't love her, this imposter, whoever he is. The only reason for his persistence is his sexual vanity, a pride that seems to drive him because he cannot endure being ignored.

Finally, Miranda talks herself into turning away from the door once and for all. She goes back to bed, feeling victorious, and falls into a nervous sleep.

Propped against white pillows, head swathed in bandages, Rudy hardly seems to be the same sad but playful boy Miranda had met a few days earlier at the Palace.

Drugged and exhausted, he gazes at her, asking:

"Remember me?"

"Of course. We spent an afternoon at Knossos. How do you feel?"

"Could be worse," he mumbles, rubbing his head. "Last you saw of me, I was riding a motor scooter. Right?"

Miranda smiles at Rudy's jaunty confidence, even now that he's in pain.

"That's not where I last saw you."

"I guess not." He makes a face. "When I was drowning. Right."

"Rudy will soon be able to travel," the doctor explains, looking at Miranda.

"That's good." Turning back to the patient, she asks: "So, are you going back to New York soon?"

"I s'pose. But I'd like to see some other islands first."

"Maybe Rudy could visit you on Korchula," the doctor suggests, with a poor show of innocence.

"Where's the other woman?" Rudy seems embarrassed by the doctor's pushiness.

"She should be here any minute. Oh, here she is!"

Divna enters with Sasha and Tamara, all three brushing crumbs from their clothing. Apparently they've bought their breakfast from a sidewalk vendor, eating it as they walked. Sasha is still chewing a hunk of bread and cheese, while Tamara sips milk from a paper cup.

Wearing a white dress with a low neck and a broad hem displaying a bright yellow Cretan design, Divna looks like an oversized angel. Miranda hugs her.

Rudy stares at Divna. "Aren't you the woman I saw in the café when the storm came?"

"Mamma, what's wrong with that boy? He looks funny."

"He's the boy who fell into the water, darling. He hurt his head when he fell. You remember, don't you?"

"When Bruno got mad and left?"

With an obviously fake cough and a wave, Rudy states, "Here we have Rose Red and Rose White. The ladies who saved me. Now, how did you happen to find me?"

"Miranda heard you hit the water."

"But before that for a long time I was lying in the bushes near the pool. I was drunk."

"I know. I think I heard you when I left the hotel. But of course I didn't know it was you. I wasn't even *sure* I heard anything."

"Mamma, why does that kid have rags on his head?"

"Keep still! Those aren't rags. They're bandages."

"When I fell into the water it was later, much later, I think."

"Yes, that was when we were coming back."

"Well, you saved my life. Thank you very much."

Divna warns, smiling, "Just don't do it again. We might not be here to pull you out."

"I felt pretty bad." Brightening, Rudy announces: "Maybe my father'll send you a reward."

"A reward! Never!" Miranda exclaims.

"That would be very generous of him."

"Oh well, maybe you can buy someone you like a present, take a trip or something. Say, there's one more thing I'd like to ask you two."

"Yes, what is it?" Miranda glances at her watch.

"What I want to know is, what were you two ladies—pardon me—*women* doing on the road to Knossos together at five o'clock in the morning?" Rudy's grin is mischievous.

"That's what Bruno wanted to know too," shrieks Tamara.

"Listen, I'm sorry. I really have to leave now," Miranda interjects. Reluctantly, she turns toward Divna. It is still hard for her to believe that they have shared the same man. How impossible! And yet.... "Will we meet again?" she asks, feeling sad that things have turned out this way. She would like to have known Divna better. To have made a real friend of her. But now it's entirely out of the question.

"I'm sure we'll see each other again," Divna promises. She reaches out and draws Miranda into her embrace, holding her tightly long enough to whisper into her ear. "Give him another chance. He's not a bad man. You can make him happy. I think he loves you."

Confused and very excited, Miranda walks quickly back to the hotel to get her bag before boarding the boat for Piraeus.

But when she is leaving, she walks into the lobby and finds Dionysios lounging in an armchair, a triumphant smile on his face. He gives her a mocking little bow. "Why didn't you at least let me talk to you last night? I could have explained so many things. I could have explained nearly everything, in fact."

"I really don't want to talk to you. Please, I have to go now."

"I know that. I've brought you a little gift. It's nothing special."

"More cheese?"

"Ha, ha. Well, I can appreciate other things besides cheese."

"That remains to be seen."

"May I kiss you goodbye?"

"If you touch me, I'll start yelling for the tourist police."

"All right, all right." Backing off, Dionysios bows again with heavy mockery and hands her an envelope.

"Thank you." Her voice is loud and rigid. Thrusting the envelope into her bag, she picks up her suitcase and walks out of the hotel. Dionysios stands with his arms folded across his chest, watching her exit.

Once she is safely on the boat sailing away from Crete, Miranda opens the envelope. Inside is a tightly folded packet of black silk, and when she unwraps it, the object turns out to be an eye mask richly embroidered with colors that glow against the black background: coppery brown, turquoise ovals containing circles of deep blue, and a pale shade of green as luminous as a cat's eye. Tied to the mask by a narrow ribbon is a note. Unfolding it, Miranda reads:

> *This mask is a gift from the artists of the past.*
> *It will help you paint. I'll soon be returning to*
> *Korchula.*
>
> *Will you still be there?*

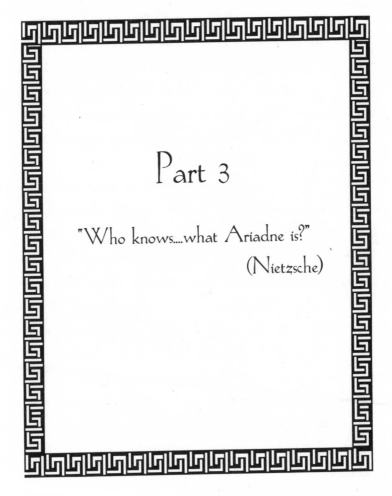

Part 3

"Who knows....what Ariadne is?"

(Nietzsche)

After Dionysios left Crete with Tamara and Sasha, and Miranda vanished too, I found myself alone, entirely alone, struggling against the apathy that we call the "Balkan malaise." I welcomed the end, absolutely, finally, of my marriage; it created a raw feeling of liberty, and yet the absence of my children left my life as untenanted as a house that has been stripped by unusually greedy and efficient thieves. I was supposed to be enjoying a month's vacation while the children stayed with their father on Korchula and in Athens, but my solitude already felt like an incurable illness.

There was the prospect of exploring the island. And there were endless and, to my way of thinking, luxuriously empty hours free for aimless reading, for reviewing parts in plays, for practicing how to make more natural-sounding phrases in English. My work was always there, with a demand to be performed, and yet I felt swollen and heavy, as though I had been swallowing small rocks and pebbles, washed down by quarts of salty water.

One day I received a telegram from Bruno. He wanted me to let him return to Crete so we could, as he put it, "try again." At first I felt a shame-faced gratitude, but I soon rejected his suggestion. I didn't feel either energetic enough to combat his peevishness or patient enough to sustain it. Supposing Bruno *did* return? We would be united for one or two nights of pleasure before he would once again feel confident of my affection and resume his chronic petulance. I yearned for Aunt Mileva's common sense and her strong hugs. My life felt full of empty holes, tears and rents, as shredded as a discarded dress. How would I pass the long sunny days of this barren month without the children, the twin anchors that prevented me from drifting toward dangerous self-pity?

I didn't bother to answer Bruno's telegram. Instead, I called Aunt Mileva in Beograd and asked her questions which made both of us laugh, about the wisdom of my final break with Dionysios (not that he would have considered resuming a relationship with me, even if that was what I wanted—the man had made it clear that he was finished with me). And, besides, now there was Miranda. I didn't know her very well but I sensed that she led a disciplined life that might provide a space where Dionysios could heal the rawness that my savagery had turned into a wound. There was a chance that these two people might be able to assuage their mutual sense of deprivation and create a strong union. He deserved an unwavering love. His losses had damaged him more than he was willing to admit, certainly to a woman.

One day I had my bags moved from the hotel to a narrow house in the town where I had rented a room for a few weeks. It was a house of old women where I was petted and teased and, generally, pampered like a little girl. Located on the third floor in the rear, my room had a long narrow balcony that

overlooked an unpretentious garden. The room itself was
draped with gaudy satins and silks. Everything was red, pink
and gold. My bed was a lushly padded mattress overhung with
a canopy of billowing red banners. On a little table beside the
bed sat a hookah. The room reminded me of the inside of a
gypsy wagon, intimate and seductive.

I especially liked the narrow balcony. Here I rested with my
arms folded on the wooden railing, staring into the garden
below where the old women grew peppers, tomatoes, corn, and
potatoes. The garden seemed ready to burst with fruits and
flowers. In one corner was a beehive; in another was a hutch for
a family of plump brown rabbits who hopped around the grass,
cavorting when they weren't sleeping in the shade, stretched
out alongside each other with a touching confidence.

Days at the house of the old women were long stretches of
nearly total idleness. I had never before known such days,
having been born in a country where hard work is taken for
granted, if a person really wants to survive. After waking up
alone in my nest of brightly colored cushions, encountering each
morning the sadness of Tamara and Sasha's absence, I would
throw on a loose robe made of flour bags that one of the women
had sewn together, and go down to the kitchen where breakfast
was always waiting: thickly sliced brown bread, butter, white
cheese, a bowl of fruit, a long-handled copper *djezvah* of
Turkish coffee, prepared the way I like it with three spoons of
sugar. There was always *ratluk* if I wanted it, and the candy
was usually offered with ironic enthusiasm by an old woman

whose teeth had long ago fallen out.

Wandering back upstairs with my cup in my hands, I would sip my coffee while watching the rabbits play. I often tried to imagine what Tamara and Sasha were doing, whether they were being taken good care of by Dionysios's mother or his stepmother, whether their diets were being properly supervised, whether they were being hugged and kissed as often as they needed these tokens of reassurance.

Lounging on my balcony, drinking sweet black coffee, I would let my mind wander through the collection of contemporary plays I had brought with me. Except for one aspect of Phaedra that I hadn't mastered and except for Medea, which my unfortunate good humor might have prohibited me from ever mastering, I had conquered the classical tragedies and was acquiring more contemporary works in which to challenge myself. I was reading European and American plays but so far I hadn't found anything that attracted me strongly enough to make me try to persuade Dushko to chance it.

Mornings were for unhurried exploratory reading as I lay across the mass of pillows the old women called a bed. The noon meal was always a feast that began with soup, no matter how hot the day, and always ended with pastries soaked in honey and filled with farina and pale cheese. After eating, I would return to my room and put on my bathing suit, covering myself with a tunic or sundress, take a basket and wander to the beach. At first these strolls were rambling. I was looking for the right spot, a private beach where I could bathe naked.

It wasn't long before I discovered the place that matched the image I'd formed in my imagination, a foam beach that was shielded from the land by a thrust of dark gray stone nearly thirty feet high, while at a distance, in the shallow water, was a rock formation a third this size, darker, jutting roughly toward the land in the shelter of the dominant precipice. Here, protected and warmed, the sea rolled into the gently sloping beach, nearly translucent, a pale shade of green. The sand was covered with shiny egg-shaped rocks, quite large and, therefore, formidable enough to keep the tourists away. Here I could splash and frolic naked as long as I felt like it, bathe or even lie in the shallow green water on my stomach. I passed long afternoons in this way, abandoned to a solitary and aimless sensuality. This way of life was new to me. At times I enjoyed it very much, but more often I felt a hollow anguish.

One day a letter came, forwarded by Aunt Mileva. It was from an American movie producer. It seemed that a young rock star had "set his heart," as the Americans say, on making a "pop" film version of "Hippolytus" with myself in the role of the crazed Phaedra. A rock version of "Hippolytus." I wouldn't have to sing, fortunately, and I'd be paid very well. This letter made me burst out laughing, the proposal was so ridiculous. And yet, I was tempted; for a long time I'd wanted to go to the U.S. and do all the silly things I'd never done before: to walk around malls staring at people, to eat Chinese food until I got sick, to sit in a beauty salon while other women washed my hair and painted my fingernails. I knew that people would ridicule me for desiring such idiotic treats. No one seemed to understand how very few innocent pleasures life had offered me so far.

When I thought of Dionysios I was, for a few seconds, nervous and then, later, just plain scared. I liked to think that by meeting the challenge of the past—its enthusiasms and its losses—I had conquered it, disposing of its power to intrude on the present. But after passing whole days in acute anxiety, I felt imprisoned without being able to say who or what had given me this feeling of bondage. Was it love that had enslaved me? I felt like one of those dolls whose brightly colored dirndl skirts conceal, on the other side of Grandma's benignly smiling face, the grimace of the wolf with his jaw full of jagged teeth.

When the fervor of anxious panting had passed, I began to take long aimless walks up and down the island's twisting roads. I climbed around the ridges that encircled the grapevines, winding around the green and gray slopes. I sat alone in the big café in the harbor, drinking coffee and occasionally eating *ratluk*.

For the time my impulse to rush off to New York subsided, and I was fairly contented, even though my loneliness had lost its sweet freshness. As I flung myself up and down the length of the island, crossing and recrossing the rocks along the rough coast, I wondered whether even if I had decided to return, I would've had the strength to go back. A mysterious engine with jagged little flywheels was clicking away inside my head. If I walked, if I read, if I wrote, I felt miserable. If I sat down alone to enjoy a dinner of grilled fish and tomato salad, I was likely to suffer a stab of fear. I thought I had healed myself of the disease of self-sufficiency.

But I was mistaken.

One night I dreamed: I am descending a stairway that disappears under the dark oily surface of a body of water that is covered by a murky gray film. The curving stone stairway vanishes in the depths of this dark water.

The stairway descends, piercing the surface of a cavern filled with dark greenish-black water. I walk slowly down the stairs; I am wearing a full skirt made of tiered flounces held at the waist by a wide golden girdle that rises under my naked breasts. On my head is a crown of intertwined serpents; my feet are bound by sandals. Slowly, I move down the stairway, moving toward the dark water.

In the darkness of the stairway strangers are waiting, waiting to caress me, waiting to plant their lips upon my flesh, drawing from it a moist sweetness, waiting to kiss open the entrances into which they might thrust their fingers and their swollen sex organs, which are taut with desire, hard in expectation of giving pleasure with long penetrating motions. Wrenching away, I continue my slow glide down along the stairway toward the dark oily surface of the water. Slowly, I descend the stairs, moving toward the bottom step where the stones disappear beneath the oily surface. Downward I glide, until one sandaled foot touches the surface of the first step that lies submerged. The current surges upward. I lose my balance, then regain it, extending my toe, groping for a foothold. I descend. The water rises, lifting my flounced skirts around my naked thighs. Rising higher, the water flows around my hips and swells upward, encircling my waist. Still, I force my body downward, pushing against the water as I thrust lower into the blackness that embraces my breasts and rises higher to my shoulders. My toe seeks the step, the last step, the toe dancing in circles in the depths of the water, circling but finding no resting place.

I stumble and fall. My face sinks beneath the surface; my body pitches forward. The heavy water fills my clothing with a rotten smell. My soaked skirts pull me farther and farther down, until I feel my mouth fill up with scum, shreds of lily pads and weeds, gritty foul-tasting water. Beating at the water with my fists, I struggle, but I cannot rise. The drenched flounces of my wide skirts pull me into the depths. Finally, the water closes over my head.

After a morning of hard work, I climb down my hill to the town for supplies: razor blades, paint remover, fresh bread and coffee, some white cheese, and a bottle of brandy. My string bag over my arm, I cross the broad sunny central plaza, smiling and nodding at the islanders. Every day I exchange an incomprehensible ritual with an ancient woman swathed in black, who often opens her window when she sees me walking through the town during the hottest time of the day. She thrusts out her head, shaking a warning finger at the blazing round mass of orange flame burning in the blue sky. But today she nods approvingly because I'm wearing dark glasses and a straw hat. As always, I stand for a while at the harbor, admiring the calm blue sea that flows into the cove of huge bone-dry white rocks, sea-smoothed slabs that form the mooring. Its motors cut, the Adriatic ferry is gliding through the glassy surface of the water. The passengers are ready to disembark, loaded with bundles, bent under the weight of backpacks or jugs of wine or burlap bags full of peppers, tomatoes and ears of yellow corn. I am waiting for Rudy, whose visit was promised weeks earlier. But I don't see him among the crowd of tourists and work-worn islanders.

At nearly three the smell of roasting goat fills the air. The outdoor café whose tiny tables are scattered around the harbor plaza is filled with diners who are breaking off hunks of bread and chewing heartily while they wait for the meat to cook and the waiters to bring plates of fried peppers in olive oil and garlic, or cucumber and lettuce salads.

The smells of the food are tempting. I stand in the sun hesitating, one hand in the pocket of my black sundress, weighing the key to my house at the top of the hill. But my waiting work is more attractive than the food and so, adjusting the brim of my straw hat, I turn away and recross the big plaza, enjoying the smooth feel of the paving stones beneath the thin soles of my sandals.

As I climb the wide stairway that leads to a smaller plaza in front of the town's Venetian-style cathedral, I hear music. Music at this time of day! I can hear the sounds of a three-piece band: drum, flute and a stringed instrument made out of a hollowed-out gourd, a *gusle*. The drum is the familiar Balkan type, an enormous object strapped to the musician's body and beaten as he walks, carrying it in front of him like an immense belly whose stretched skin he pounds with sticks held tightly in both fists. In this way he can comfortably march with the other musicians from one village to another, providing entertainment in the rough cobbled streets, afterward passing around a battered tin cup. Sometimes, dancing bears lumber alongside these meandering musicians, moving their shaggy bodies to the slow mournful banging of the drum. The rhythm, the melody, the tone: all are heavy, laden with a lament that is Balkan to the last throb. Today, this band of three musicians is playing a war dance while, in the flat sunny area in front of the cathedral, a group of local men are slowly moving in a circle, stamping their feet to the rhythm of the drum.

Naked to the waist, the men hold both arms upraised as they move; in their fists they clench short, thick-bladed swords. As the drum pounds, the men circle, arms uplifted, swords held in the air. The swords clash. The men resume their circling. Again, a pause and the swords clank. The circle of men turns. A pause. The swords clash. As the dancers move, the rhythm quickens, the beats of the huge drum closer and closer together. The clashing of the swords becomes louder, the rhythm grows faster, steel striking steel. The tension increases. The dancers wheel, strike, wheel, strike, wheel and strike, wheel and strike. The pace becomes so rapid it seems violent.

Watching, I lose myself in a trance. The dancers continue to wheel and strike their swords together. Then, they pause. The clashing of the metal swords rings out. Faster still, they move, turning and striking, making a harsh and brutal music with their perspiring bodies. A drop of thick red blood falls onto the stones of the plaza.

"Someone's cut!" exclaims a voice at my back, a familiar voice. It's Rudy's voice. And there he stands, looking healthy, tanned, a backpack on the ground beside him.

"I thought I'd never find you!" He grins.

"Rudy! It's great to see you! I really thought you'd changed your mind and you weren't coming."

"Nope! Here I am! What's going on here?"

"It's just a dance. How long can you stay?"

"Oh, not long. I have to go back. School's starting soon."

"Let's have some coffee. There's a café right here."

We sit down, and Rudy exclaims:

"Hey, you look great, Miranda! Got over your love affair, I guess."

"Actually, no I haven't."

"Hey, who're these guys dancing?"

"Just the local men." Among them, I recognize the vendor of red wine, the man who walks up and down the plaza selling snacks of olives wrapped in paper cones, the man who owns a butcher shop where he presides over cases of raw lamb and pork, the man who sells cigarettes, gum, and *ratluk* on a tray suspended from his neck, the man who delivers the mail, riding all over the island on a girl's battered red bike, and the man who—I am unable to figure out his schedule—stands in the center of the large plaza opposite the harbor wearing a dirty white uniform and enormous dress gloves; his job is to make the German tourists drive more slowly lest they kill, besides pigs, sheep and goats, the islanders themselves.

"So the Greek's still in the picture! What a disappointment!" Rudy waves at the proprietor, a heavy man who is standing nearby with his arms folded across his stomach. He is wearing a dirty apron. Since I never order anything but coffee, he's in no rush to wait on us.

But when he comes finally with a brass tray holding two small cups of Turkish coffee, the man is friendly. He offers us an explanation of the sword dance:

"It is very old, this dance. It is called the 'Mareshka.' No one knows its origin. It is performed no place in the world except on Korchula and also on Sardinia."

We nod; to me it feels very good to have a companion, even if he is only fourteen.

The proprietor rubs the apron that partially covers his bulging stomach, and his smile is tender as he says: "These dancers are ordinary islanders like me. We keep the dance alive. The old men teach it to the young men."

We watch as the dancers put on the shirts hanging from the branches of a lime tree that grows in front of the cathedral.

"Miranda, I need to eat. All they had on the ferry was some bitter wine."

With a benevolent grunt the proprietor agrees to provide a plate of roasted goat with horseradish and steamed carrots and potatoes. It's obvious that he considers this meal a very fine one. Therefore, when I see a look of dismay appear on Rudy's face, I kick him lightly under the table.

"That'll be fine," I tell the man. Tourists from the U.S., I've observed, accept practically every other inconvenience with good humor, even the infamous Turkish toilet. But they get nasty only when told with finality that there are no beefsteaks on the island, only goat.

The wine loosens our laughter; it's pleasant to sit in the sunlight sharing a meal with someone who's easy to talk to, and I feel a great distance from the obsessed and lonely woman who lives on the nearby hill.

Rudy leans near me and asks a surprising question:

"Miranda, what does 'deniaiser' mean? In French?"

"Well, of course in French." I laugh. "Rudy, who taught you that word?"

"Can't you guess?"

"We'll talk about it later," I say with pretended sternness. Actually, I'm amused at Rudy's hint at a mutual new experience. His doctor must have put him up to this charade.

"Tell me something, Rudy, when are you going to be fifteen?"

We're laughing and drinking wine when a man, a whistling man, quickly rounds the corner and walks past our table. At the sight of Rudy and me, this man stops and nods abruptly. It's Dionysios.

Rudy giggles.

"I've come back."

"So we see."

Still whistling, one hand in his pocket, he walks away just as if he hasn't even *seen* Rudy and me, let alone announced his return.

"Well," Rudy offers, "I know you have things to do, and I'm really sleepy. I was seasick on the boat. But if you're not doing anything tomorrow morning, maybe we can go to the beach."

"Okay. The best beach is at the Hotel Park. It's just around the bend in the harbor."

"See you there at about ten tomorrow."

"Okay." I pick up my string bag full of tomatoes and peppers. "Sleep well, Rudy. I've got a lot of work to do."

The next day Rudy and I meet on the beach at the Hotel Park but it is very crowded. Tourists are sprawled everywhere; oily bodies are draped over all the rocks and lounge chairs. The water is speckled with the heads of the bathers.

"I can't stand this crowd," Rudy complains. "Isn't there a more secluded part?"

And so I lead him up a rocky slope, around a bend, down a long narrow dusty road, and through a cornfield until we reach a private beach I discovered one afternoon during a walk around the island. Spreading out my towel, I lie back and close my eyes.

"Don't disturb yourself," Rudy says. "I'm going for a swim."

"How funny New York is going to seem," I mumble, half-asleep.

Rudy retorts, "Hey, what makes you think you're going back to New York? You're going to marry that scowling Greek. You'll give up painting and have five or six scowling brats."

"Oh shut up!"

Later, I'm not sure how much later, I awaken slowly, drowsily from the deep distance of a nap. Rudy is lying beside me, playing with my hair. He kisses my shoulder, then curls up against my back with his face buried in the nape of my neck, nuzzling a little, like a baby. His sex is hard as he rocks against my body, rubbing himself even larger. For a moment I am shocked, and I hesitate, muttering at him to stop. But then another impulse, a simple desire, overwhelms my censor. I lie quietly, just waiting; all that's needed is a relaxed willingness. Rudy seems quite capable of finishing what he's started and I am glad that he lies behind me, unable to see the smile with which I celebrate his initiation. On my part it is an act of friendship—not altogether an unselfish one. I think to myself— have I absorbed some of Divna's boldness?

Afterward, Rudy rolls onto his back and giggles.

I sit up and comb my hair with my fingers, leaning back on my arms with my face toward the sky. I'm not ready to look at him.

"Miranda, that was very sweet. Thank you very much, old girl." Yawning, he drops back onto the sand. "You're a good friend."

"When're you going back to New York, boyfriend?" I want him to understand that nothing more is going to happen.

"Oh gosh! Tomorrow. Or the next day. I'd rather stay here."

"But you can't."

When we climb up to my house, three gypsy women are sitting on the stones. Like brilliantly colored flowers blown onto the grass from an overgrown garden, they seem to rise from the centers of their cushiony skirts like the petals of flamboyant blossoms. Black curls float around their faces. In their black eyes I read amusement and mischief. When they smile their mouths reveal fortunes of gold.

As I greet them the women shake out their skirts and sway
to their feet. They are barefoot. Above their many skirts they
are wearing tight synthetic sweaters adorned with myriad
chains of gold coins, which allow the movement of their bodies
to make music.

Rudy stares. "What savage beauties!" he exclaims.
"Dirty—but gorgeous!"

The youngest woman steps forward and takes a tiny piece of
paper from a pouch attached to her belt of gold coins. "Read
later," the gypsy directs as she hands the note to me with a
roguish look. Grinning and bowing, she backs away, pulling the
other women with her. Swaying and jingling like big heavy
bells, they walk off into the distance.

"What's your note say?" Rudy prods. "It's got to be from
Omar, Achilles, Apollo or whatever that damned Greek's name
is."

"Will you shut up!" I laugh. "You're right. His mother's a
gypsy." The note reads:

> *Love is only possible in a strange country.*
> *If you want to love really, you must begin*
> *a new life....*

I burst out laughing. "Oh Rudy, what'll I do?"

Rudy shrugs and brushes some sand from his wrist. A little
sullen, he snaps: "How do I know? Anyway, what do I care? I'm
going back to New York tomorrow."

One morning I realized that my final impetuous sex with Dionysios had made me pregnant. The obvious solution was readily available in any clinic, and there was plenty of time. A voluptuous, even an obviously pregnant Phaedra would present no one with a problem, not in this part of the world, and by the time I decided to go to the States to make the movie, *if* I decided to do this, my body would have returned to normal. If the father had been Bruno I wouldn't have hesitated, but the father wasn't Bruno. In fact, I had no enthusiasm for getting rid of my pregnancy. I simply shoved this problem under a hundred less important ones.

I was leaning on the balcony one morning, sipping coffee and watching the rabbits leap around on the grass, when I saw—or thought I saw—something moving in the bushes, perhaps a bird or a rabbit. But I was mistaken about what caused the foliage to rustle. First, a blond head was thrust between the growth of a large oleander plant. Next, a young man emerged from the bushes and stood staring up at me. It was his face that first attracted me and, later, his lithe body, of medium height, a body that was subtly, almost discreetly modeled. His face was long and oval, a shade of golden beige that was not native to this island nor to any other part of the Adriatic, Aegean or Libyan Seas. His eyes were pale gray, his nose straight, his lips short, full, rounded, shaped for sensuality. The hair that grew thickly on his chest and forearms was golden. Wearing cut-off jeans, he was barefoot and bare-headed. He smiled up at me, reminding me of a Nordic night ablaze. Certainly, he was no Greek.

Feeling stupid, for I was momentarily mesmerized, I returned his stare before I called out—idiotically—"Hi!"

His lips opened but no sounds emerged. Instead, a quick spasm seized his features, wrenching them into an expression of frustrated pain. Swiftly turning, the man disappeared into the banks of greenery, but not before he had flung me a wave, delicately, as if shaking it from slender fingers with an interesting reluctance to let go of the gesture.

Shaking my head, I wondered whether I had seen a vision, a faun or a satyr, a creature who had escaped from the woods and found himself confused by the city. Of course. I knew that in reality he was probably just a shy and inarticulate boy. The role of Phaedra had confused me.

Toward sundown when the island is transformed for a brief time into a cloudy mass of delicate rose light, and the sea sways in the harbor as if murmuring an evening song to the tired fishermen, toward sundown a little more than a month after my return to Korchula, I find myself walking down the big hill with an excited heart but uncertain feet. I am trying to carry a large painting, clutching it in front of my body with both arms. It's a gift for the gypsy Esma, whose son has, with strange formality, invited me to dinner at her house.

I haven't seen Dionysios since he ran into Rudy and me a few days earlier with such a ridiculous display of jealousy. And then, that note, its silliness! But he enjoys these games, and so do I.

Very uncomfortable because of the awkwardness of managing the painting, I am wearing my favorite red and gold East Indian print dress with wide full sleeves. My work has been going well too. The paintings come quickly and are finished quickly. Besides, I am looking forward to the dinner. Island life, no matter how lovely the island, can be lonely.

As I pass through the sun-warmed streets I can feel the heat through the worn soles of my sandals. Smiling and nodding, I greet the townspeople, moving clumsily past the "Non-Stop," the island's supermarket from which satisfied, triumphant tourists are emerging with bags of bottled and canned food.

The plaza is filled with local people who, largely because they can't afford the prices at the "Non-Stop," carry string bags stuffed with raw vegetables and loaves of crusty brown bread.

As usual on this long, mild, rose-tinted afternoon when I make an appearance in the town, especially if I'm wearing something that seems unusual to the islanders, I am followed by a horde of laughing shrieking gypsy children, looking like battered blossoms in their gaudy rags. This afternoon three or four little girls are trailing behind me, attracted by my red and gold dress and by the long Mexican earrings that hang nearly to my shoulders. Marveling at such wealth, the children don't know that my earrings are just tin dipped in gold paint, a "jewel" available to tourists for about seventy-five cents in the public square of Oaxaca in Mexico.

On the outside, Esma's house is indistinguishable from the island's other houses: a narrow three-storey building tucked into a street not more than eight or ten feet wide. An emblem on the carved wooden door is the only detail that distinguishes this house from its neighbors. There is a brass knocker shaped like a panther's head. The eyes of the beast are immense and totally empty of expression; his lips are drawn back in a menacing snarl that reveals two rows of murderous-looking teeth. Around the panther's neck hangs a wreath woven of grape leaves festooned with clusters of fruit. In legends, the panther always accompanies Dionysios.

In spite of the unsettling effect of this object on my nerves, I raise the knocker and let it fall three times.

I wait, wondering why I am not afraid to encounter the man who has caused me so much suffering.

The door is opened by a child about nine or ten years old. He is wearing a brightly embroidered tunic and a wide red sash tied over his loose Turkish-style black pants. On his feet are the soft leather slippers with curled-up toes, the *opanci* that the peasants wear. Unsmiling but not, I feel, unfriendly, the boy leads me past the open door of a very large kitchen in which I glimpse a long trencher table, a huge coal stove and a wooden cupboard lacquered red. The kitchen is filled with ancient gypsy women bent over their work, most with cigarettes between their lips; they seem oblivious to the pleading of the flocks of children who hang on their bunched-up colored skirts. As I pass, still lugging the huge canvas in my aching arms, I cannot help but smile at the crones' exclamations: *"Ameri-kanka!"*

I follow the child up a short flight of steep smoothly-worn stone stairs to a small sitting room on the second floor. Here, a heap of brightly colored pillows lies in disarray on a well-worn silky-looking Persian carpet. Beside a dark red puff of an ottoman stands a low table made of ebony and decorated with arabesques of inlaid ivory and mother-of-pearl. The walls are a pale shade of violet, and across their unthreatening expanse bright blue fish are soaring with amazing energy, or maybe they aren't fish but dolphins. Relieved to get rid of the painting, I drop onto the ottoman and rub my arms to smooth away the indentations left by the canvas.

While resting, I can look over the room's most interesting feature: a stained glass window portraying a little girl, her chubby arms overflowing with a bouquet of lilies. The setting sun irradiates this image with surprising brilliance.

From the floor above comes the sound of the usual energetic Balkan music—heavy drumming, the rhythmic clinking of a tambourine, punctuated by the honks of some sort of brass instrument.

Esma introduces her two children: her son Radovan, and her daughter, Rosalba. She adds, "I think you've at least *met* Sasha and Tamara on the beach in Crete." Then, with an insinuating wink, she concludes, "You already know my oldest son."

Dionysios barely glances at me, for Tamara is clinging to his right hand, Sasha to his left. The children produce brief nasty smiles for me, their innocent jealousy undisguised. But Esma breaks the mood by taking the children from Dionysios and seating them at the table.

Without further conversation we sit down, Esma opposite the four children, myself at one end of the table and Dionysios at the other. With the fierce light of the sunset at his back, blurring his features in radiance, he seems more a phantom than a man. I risk an incongruity: A Mozartian joke, as I quip:

"*Cos'e tal mascherata?*"

"So you know Italian," replies Esma, whose response I had not expected, while Dionysios, whom I hoped to bait with my allusion to Mozart's opera of ridiculous disguises, frowns almost gravely, turning away from me. As his face turns, the light illuminates his features so brilliantly that I am startled, with the same force as on the first day of our meeting, by the changeable gray shade of his eyes, a gray that is intensified by black eyelashes and heavy brows.

"My son is moody," Esma apologizes, with a friendly pat. "I know the Italian language when I hear it, but I do not understand the words. What does that mean: *'Cos'e tal mascherata'*?"

Glancing at me with caution, Dionysios risks a barely perceptible smile of pride in his mother's knowledge as well as her honesty.

"It means, 'what's going on here, some sort of masquerade?'"

Esma laughs heartily. "You have a good sense of humor! Good! Teach *him* how to laugh," she commands with a nod at her first-born. Radovan and Rosalba begin to giggle, poking each other with their fists as they chew on crusts of bread. The burgundy-colored tablecloth is already littered with crumbs. Radovan pries a piece of bread from between his front teeth with his finger. Esma slaps his wrist and whispers an order of some sort into Rosalba's ear. Rosalba and Radovan quickly disappear into the kitchen. Sasha eats with focused concentration, but Tamara barely touches her food. Her eyes are fastened on her father, a look of molten resentment. I wonder, is it my presence that has provoked her unhappiness? Her expression is almost a sulk.

"Children!" Esma proclaims with a laugh. Looking directly at Tamara, she says, "They're usually not as much trouble as their fathers, but trouble all the same."

Tamara does not appear to absorb this gentle and impersonally framed rebuke.

"The children are beautiful," I quickly counter, with a spontaneous generosity that I regret when I see the smile of amused triumph it brings to the face of my one-time island lover. "And Tamara looks exactly like her mother," I add. "A pink and rose cherub. Sasha, hmm...he seems a perfect combination of his parents." This effort to disperse the sense of clotted discomfort is successful.

"Yes, they are beautiful," assents Esma. "Even *him*."

Vigorously, I nod, sensing that once I've won Esma's good will there is no possibility of making a mistake; if there are rules of decorum in this household, a person would have to be a very frequent visitor to discover them. I loosen up with the assurance that when Esma is in command, whatever is natural will pass with approval. She is freer than her son and maybe more intelligent too. If not more intelligent, more adventurous. As for Dionysios, he is becoming even more mysterious than he seemed months earlier. Now I am beginning to glimpse beneath his surface of playful humor, a raw, almost bitter, and certainly resentful sense of having been wounded.

Rosalba and Radovan return on tiptoes, Rosalba carrying a huge tureen of soup.

Esma spoons the succulent smelling soup into large bowls and says something quickly to Radovan.

Suddenly, Rosalba and Radovan raise their high voices and

begin singing, in a nearly incomprehensible English, Maurice Sendak's litany in praise of chicken soup. Smiling, I praise their pronunciation and repeatedly pat their shoulders, wishing that Esma would serve more wine. The soup is a rich creamy blend of cauliflower, butter and yogurt, inviting me to devour it with unashamed gusto, an act that brings a happy smile to Esma's face. Radovan and Rosalba make slurping noises as they spoon the hot soup into their mouths. Dionysios shoots the children a look of disapproval.

Everyone seems to be having a good time except Dionysios and his daughter. As for Sasha, he is so quiet it's hard to know what he's feeling. Missing his mother, probably. And I imagine that Divna must be missing her children deeply. Now she is alone on Crete....I am not sure why, except that she said this period of solitude was what she needed.

Dionysios turns to me and asks in a whimsical dreamy tone whether I'm enjoying myself. Tamara's eyes flash back and forth between us, not so much with hostility as with uneasy curiosity.

Long seconds pass before I answer. In a country where staring at other people is the principal form of entertainment, I feel wholly justified in letting my eyes rest on his saturnine face, a face of seductive beauty, dominated by a large, high-bridged nose, and swollen, almost sulky lips that express uneasy discontent as well as a formidable sensuality.

Excusing themselves, Radovan and Sasha disappear and reappear with the main course, a lamb and cabbage stew liberally seasoned with real paprika. Now lots of red wine is served. I drink a lot, letting the children fill my glass many times.

The children smack their lips and slurp as they eat, adding the music of enjoyment to the dinner. Esma eats with the same innocent pleasure as her children, jingling her many rings and bangles as she lifts her hand to her mouth. When we've finished the stew we relax with cups of Turkish coffee and plates of pastries. With a nod toward Esma, who's cleaning her teeth with one hand, shielding this action from our eyes with the other, Dionysios turns to me with an ironic smile that is matched by the discomfort in his eyes.

"After the joke I played, I owe you an explanation, don't I? Divna told you Esma's my mother."

Nodding, I wait for him to unfold his story while he fortifies himself with a long drink of wine.

"She was only twelve when I was born. My father is a businessman in Athens. So I'm half-Greek. Radovan and Rosalba have different fathers too."

Esma interjects, winks boldly at me before raising a telling finger to the side of her head.

"Of course, to you Dionysios is an absurd name. To any non-Greek it must seem like a joke to have a name like that." Another long drink of wine seems to loosen his words; he speaks more quickly, with less overt concern. His pride in his mother is obvious.

"Now we go upstairs for music and dancing," Esma

commands. "Come on!"

She takes Tamara and Sasha by the hand while Radovan and Rosalba follow.

There's no possibility of refusing.

Almost shyly, Dionysios draws me toward the door with a gaze that is tentative, almost demure. For some reason he seems inhibited, maybe because he is without his mask. For unmasked, he can no longer participate in the masquerade of our former days.

One day the old women decided that the house needed cleaning. They took down all the curtains, the fabrics that decorated the walls, dismantled the pillow beds, and gathered up all the dirty clothing. Heaps of dirty stuff were piled onto a red wooden wagon. The old man who sometimes worked in the house or garden helped, leading a small mahogany-colored mare which he harnessed to the wagon. The old man, as well as the women, tied flowered scarves over their heads and topped these off with straw hats. They invited me to go with them, and I accepted, pulling on a shapeless black dress tied at the waist with a piece of rope and covering my hair with a red scarf decorated with coins. Underneath, I wore my swimming suit.

We formed a procession of about fifteen: myself, the old man, six or seven women and half a dozen children who followed us for the fun of it. We passed through the center of town with a somber air that was hardly justified by the nature of the outing. The tourists were dismayed. They stopped, stared and pointed their cameras at us. Some of the old women grumbled but others grinned at the foreigners. The children assumed grotesque poses and made faces, thumbing their ears or their noses at the island's visitors, mostly Germans and Americans, French and Italians.

When we had crossed the town we moved through a narrow

sandy road to the coast, meandering over a flat even stretch that the horse could manage and where the water was shallow, cool and clear enough for washing. The mare was quite frisky and had to be gently restrained. What if she decided to bolt with a wagon full of dirty laundry! The old man kept his hand on the harness, tapping a set of brass bells so that we had a jingling accompaniment to the old women's chattering. The children ran and skipped, reciting nonsense poems in a made-up mysterious language. Once outside the town, I took off my sandals, letting my feet sink into the sandy earth. I enjoyed the oozing sound.

Finally, the old man brought us to a long flat place where we could wash the clothes. He rolled up his pant legs and led the mare straight into the water, the wagon bumping slightly. We women bunched our skirts up around our waists, securing them by tucking them into our belts. The old man's presence didn't bother the women at all. After all, one of them shouted at him, at his age he'd seen everything, including her own skinny flanks. This made the others hoot. The children scattered in all directions as they chased one another, shouting and laughing.

Bare-legged, we stood in the water dunking the soiled clothing and scrubbing it with bars of yellow soap. For me it wasn't at all hard work. Some of us sang as we scrubbed. One had brought a washboard and she dashed the dirty clothes against it with a pretense of violence. When everything had been washed, the women gathered wood and built a fire on the beach, neatly stacking the logs in a cross shape. They rolled a metal barrel from the wagon bed, tumbled it on its side and filled it with water. Then, tugging and pulling, they dragged the barrel over to the crossed logs and hoisted it onto the fire. When the water boiled, they filled the barrel with sheets and pillowcases. I helped them haul the heavy water-logged stuff out of the water and lift the dripping clothes into a barrel of bleach. It was strange to see the fire blaze up against the sunny sky.

When everything had been rinsed and wrung out and the white things were boiling away in the cauldron, the women sat back on the sand, gossiping. A few squatted the way they do in the marketplace, leaning on their heels, their wares spread in front of them. Some smoked brown cigarettes that they rarely touched with their hands once they'd put them between their lips and started to puff. Some of the women didn't talk at all, but just sat quietly crouching or napping.

Deciding to go around the bend to swim a little, I walked back into the water, my skirts still bunched up around my waist, and headed for a formation of steep gray rocks on the other side of the cove. When I reached the spot, carefully climbing over slippery rocks, I found a scrap of beach that was totally unapproachable because it was cut off from the land by sharp cliffs. The water was translucent, a pale aquamarine, and it became quite deep not far from the shore. I noted this carefully, for as much as I loved the water, I was not an expert swimmer, as I'd learned when Miranda and I had gone in to save the drowning boy.

Laying my dress on a rock and stripping off my bathing suit,
I walked into the sea with a morsel of soap in my hand, not the
harsh yellow laundry soap of the washwomen but a sliver of
creamy soap with a rose scent that I had saved from the Hotel
Xenia. I swam out, not far, turned onto my back and floated
idly, my eyes closed. After a while I stroked back toward the
inlet into which the surf rushed with a brisk energy. My
vacation, I thought with a laugh, I was spending it washing
dirty laundry with a flock of old women!

Standing up, I soaped myself carefully all over, bending and
balancing on one foot while I washed the other. When I was
ready to rinse, I stooped down and splashed the cool water into
my face and over my shoulders and breasts. Finally, after I'd
rinsed off all the suds and foam, I stood up again and rubbed
what remained of the soap into my hair. Ducking my head
under the water several times, I worked up a fine lather. I was
rubbing my head energetically, feeling rather mindlessly happy,
when I heard the engine of a motorboat. A large cabin cruiser
was approaching the inlet, moving too fast for me to get my
dress back on. The boat came quite close to me. On the deck
were two men and a woman. One of the men was holding a
pair of binoculars through which he was observing me. I was so
startled, I tried to cover myself, one hand flying to my pubic
hair, the other to my breasts.

I thought that once they saw me, the people on the boat
would retreat. I was mistaken. Instead they cut the motor and
the cruiser idled, giving the people on deck a chance to continue

staring at me. I yelled at them to move. But they wouldn't, not even when I took my hand off my breasts and shook my fist at them. Finally, I had no choice but to turn my back and walk as calmly as possible to the rocks where I'd left my clothing. I refused to hurry. With absolute deliberation I bent down and shook out my dress, pulling it on with leisurely purposefulness. When I'd tied my belt and fluffed my hair around my face so it would dry, I put my basket over my arm and started walking back around the bend. The cabin cruiser followed me, slowly.

The women were gathering everything together for our return, folding the damp clothes and stacking them on the wagon. The strangers kept on watching us, protected by their powerful boat. The children came running back to the wagon, flying across the beach like gaily colored banners. One of the old women carried a bucket of sea water to the fire and doused it. The cauldron was tumbled onto its side, lifted and put back on the wagon bed.

We were ready. We re-tied our scarves and replaced our straw hats, watching the old man lead the mare out of the water. She came prancing, legs lifted high, delicately, proudly, harness bells jingling.

On the way back to town I began to reconsider my desire to go to the United States. What sort of welcome would I receive there? Would I be stared at like a robust primitive?

I decided that I shouldn't go too far from my own territory. Otherwise, I'd just be another curiosity.

The next evening I was invited to have dinner with some visiting tourists, an American producer of stage shows and his wife, maybe others too. I was to come to their yacht in the harbor to discuss the possibility of our working together. Very pleased, I accepted, hoping that it might lead to an offer to perform something truly dignified.

I wore a white cotton dress with a rounded neckline, let my hair loose, pulling it back to one side with a gardenia. I wanted to create an ambiguous appearance, partly innocent and partly flamboyant. Knowing that so many people think I'm a simple-minded savage, I decided to exploit this impression as I had exploited the other roles life had foisted on me. I walked through the streets of the town to the bay where wealthy people from all over the world moored their yachts. Here, in the early evenings, it was common to see expensive boats bobbing slightly while their owners sat aboard at dinner tables on which candles burned, throwing weird lights on the deeply tanned faces of the rich who appeared totally undisturbed by the envious or simply curious stares of the islanders as they passed, just leaving work or shopping for groceries. Phrases of French, English, Spanish, Italian, and German drifted on the evening air, along with the fragile sounds of glass and china grazing each other as dishes of food were circulated by perfectly manicured hands. On the largest of these pleasure boats white jacketed waiters were moving about. The finest stereos provided the boring tunes that Americans call "dinner music."

On one of these boats I was greeted by the producer, whose name was Howard Monroe, and his wife Letty. A chicly thin woman with long straight blonde hair and dry over-tanned skin, Letty was seated in a deck chair, her legs crossed. In her hand she held a glass of transparent liquid in which ice tinkled. Letty Monroe was wearing a short navy blue tennis dress. No jewelry except for diamonds—I suppose they were diamonds that glittered in her ears—becoming visible when she flipped her long hair back over her shoulders. Her fingernails were ruby red. On her face was an expression of chronic disturbance, but maybe it was just unhappiness. Her voice reminded me of the sound of the ice in her glass.

Howard Monroe was agreeably tall and thin, in cool and confident possession of polished and rather synthetic good looks. In contrast to his wife, he was dark. When I arrived he was wearing green swimming trunks in a luminous fabric. Drops of water clung to his oiled skin, making him look like a seal. As soon as he made sure I had seen his nearly naked body, Howard Monroe excused himself and went below to change.

Crouched on the deck in the shadows was a young man whom Letty Monroe introduced as her son. Somehow I wasn't especially surprised to recognize him as the incarnation of my garden vision, the shy boy in the cut-off jeans. Tonight he was wearing white cotton pants, but his chest was bare and on his head was a straw hat with a wide sweeping brim, a woman's hat worn with an air of obstinacy. From under the curving brim of his hat the boy gazed at me with expressionless gray eyes, which were protected by thick curling lashes. I returned his stare, a little troubled by the look that I at first thought conveyed nothing at all, but which actually expressed a profound melancholy tinged with despair. The brim of his hat called my attention to something I might not have noticed otherwise. His ears were slightly pointed and covered with fine golden hairs. His name was Gerard.

Returning to the deck, Howard Monroe asked his wife if she'd like another drink. His tone was sharp and abrupt, as though he wanted to break through the intense mood established by Gerard's expressive silence.

"More vodka," Letty Monroe said, shifting her weight as she crossed her legs even higher. Passing her, Howard Monroe smiled and brushed his hand briefly against his wife's cheek while staring at me. Letty gave him a glance filled with so much gratitude that I winced inwardly.

"Madame Divna, let me get you a drink." Turning, Howard Monroe greeted a young couple in jeans who were about to come aboard, friends of Gerard's, I supposed. The man was carrying a guitar. I thought they looked nervous, but the fact that there were other guests lessened my growing sense of discomfort. They were introduced as Rosalie and Dean.

I accepted a glass of wine. As he put it in my hand, Howard

Monroe dropped his eyes to the neckline of my dress. "You've met my wife's son," he said in a harsh voice.

"Yes. Actually, we've met before," I answered, expecting Gerard's affirmation. But he didn't respond. In fact, he didn't seem to have heard me. He suddenly thrust out his hand and seized my fingers with an urgency that alarmed me.

"That's enough," Howard said smoothly, tugging Gerard's arm. As he released my hand, Gerard's head dropped slightly to one side. I thought of a flower on a broken stalk.

Rosalie and Dean were sitting on the deck with their arms clasped around their bent knees. They were talking to Letty when Howard passed them large glasses of chilled white wine. Gerard ignored them.

I waited for Howard to raise the subject of the project he had in mind for me in the States, but he didn't say a word about it. "I've planned a nice evening," he assured us. "We're going down the coast to a marvelously primitive fish restaurant."

"'Marvelously primitive,'" I noted. Weren't we cute! We sipped our drinks as the boat glided along, moving slowly past the island's Venetian-style buildings. I watched the shadows of the trees flickering and changing shapes as the light altered. Shadows mottled the rocks that jutted out of the sea. Masses of purple clouds made the sky seem afflicted with a steadily spreading bruise. I sat quietly, waiting for Howard to broach the subject of his project. But mostly the Monroes talked about the eccentricities of my kinsmen, the islanders, who unintentionally antagonized them by their independent attitudes and their refusal to be awed by money.

Howard Monroe incessantly passed back and forth in front of my chair, deliberately displaying his trim hard body. Once he accused me of being "mysterious." Of course, I laughed. Once in a while Rosalie glanced at me curiously, as if wondering what I was doing here, just as I was wondering the same thing about her and Dean.

During all this time Gerard was staring at me with the fixed attention of a cat about to spring on a bird and tear it to shreds of bones and feathers. If I hadn't been trained to remain poised when being stared at, I would have been desperate to escape his gaze in which there was something not fully human. I saw that trapped inside of Gerard's beautiful form was a soul consumed by grief. Pity for his forced silence and his captivity stirred in me, but I tried to suppress my emotion.

Letty was a little drunk. Perched on the edge of her chair with her glass bobbing, she mindlessly repeated a crude sexual joke, insisting on Dean's response. Her tennis dress had ridden up and her thighs were spread in a way that called blatant attention to the hunger I had noticed earlier. When he looked at his wife Howard Monroe's face expressed disgust unsoftened by concern or tenderness.

It was dark when we turned into the large cove where the restaurant was located, a place I knew very well and had often visited, though I didn't tell the Monroes this. Loops of red and blue lights outlined the restaurant, and their reflections lay quietly on the water. While Howard Monroe gave his attention to mooring the cabin cruiser, Dean gave me an inquiring look with raised eyebrows. He had a fresh idealistic face.

The boat was moored in shallow water. Taking off our shoes, we waded ashore, our motions disturbing the smooth surface on which the circles of light had previously lain in serenity. Howard and Letty led the way, Dean and Rosalie following, while I came behind, childishly splashing. The only enjoyable part of this evening so far was the feel of the warm sea on my bare feet and legs. Behind me trailed Gerard. He gave off palpable vibrations of unappeased longing. It seemed to me that I could feel his breath on the back of my neck. Rather quickly, I turned once and caught him with his hand raised a few inches from my hair. In his eyes was an expression of terrified desire. It was at this moment that I understood for the first time that Gerard could not speak.

Ahead, Letty tried to whisper into Howard's ear, but when she brought her face close to his, he turned away suddenly, leaving her open lips to brush the air.

The restaurant was a ruin, a shell of rubble and small stones that had once been a village church. One wall had crumbled into a trail of boulders. The floor was tightly packed sand that had been swept into a flat surface. Overhead, the sky was dark, the moon in hiding, obscured by masses of swirling clouds. At one end of this space was a roof of plaited reeds supported by wooden poles; here the proprietor and his wife kept their supplies and did the cooking. There was a tiny bar furnished with rattan stools and an old-fashioned jukebox

whose bright neon-studded front glittered at us like a familiar
friend. But the jukebox wasn't working. There were no other
customers; most tourists didn't know about this place.

The double circle of lights, those above our heads and their
reflections, lying quietly on the sea, gave the effect of a halo
that sheltered us with encircling incandescence. The sea was
calm, swaying with a soft whisper in the cadence of a lullaby.
In such a beautiful place, I thought, people should be wildly
happy.

Even though I maneuvered for a place next to Rosalie and
Dean, Howard Monroe succeeded in guiding me into a chair
wedged between himself and his stepson. Gerard had taken off
his straw hat, revealing his long oval head. His fair curls clung
like a cap. To distract myself from the diffuse and inarticulate
emotions that seemed to emanate from him, I drank wine and
concentrated on looking at the stone wall that loomed toward
the dark sky a short distance from the restaurant. The dark
night, the ruined wall, this human gloom, were disturbing. Now
that he was sitting so close, Gerard no longer looked at me
with unbroken attention, but gazed off at the water on which
the lights lay reflected.

Taking a pillbox from her bag, Letty Monroe washed down
several pellets with a gulp of wine. Her husband watched,
frowning. Glancing across the table, I caught Rosalie's eye.
Abruptly, Dean excused himself and left the table, disappearing in the dark.

While Dean was absent, the proprietor served our dinner: a

large salad of chopped tomatoes, peppers and onions drenched in seasoned oil, platters of fried fish, baskets of bread, several more bottles of wine.

But I was too disturbed to eat. While Letty struggled with the bones in her fish, Howard insisted on deboning Rosalie's, ignoring her protests. Dean came back to the table, looking pale and ill. At my side Gerard sat, eating at a slow methodical pace, ignoring the rest of us. He seemed utterly alone.

In addition to the sight and odors of the food, Gerard's intense isolation increased my nausea. My awareness of the feelings he was unable to articulate threatened me. I had to leave the group for awhile. Excusing myself, I walked across the beach to the water, concentrating on the patterns made by the lights of the launch as it rode the gently rising and falling waves. With despair, I thought of a devastated beach I had seen earlier in the summer, the sand littered with unmated rubber sandals, dismembered limbs of dolls, scraps of rubber tires and beach balls, cracked shells, matted bunches of seaweed gummy with black tar. Lifting my skirt, I walked into the water. I could not dismiss my awareness of Gerard nor could I deny the violence of his appeal. I felt that I was being summoned to another world, and I did *not* feel like struggling against this summons, however sinister.

It wasn't long before the others came straggling down the beach. Rosalie and Dean moving quickly, almost skipping with obvious relief at the nearness of escape, I thought. Unashamedly drunk, Howard and Letty Monroe followed with fumbling steps, muttering to each other. He gave me a bleary smile and tried to take my arm to help me back into the boat, but I shook off his hand.

Back on the launch, I found a niche on the deck beside a coil of rope. There I sat, leaning back with my eyes closed. With what relief I heard the sputtering of the motors and the forward surge as the launch leaped into motion. After a while, Dean began to strum his guitar. He plucked gently at the strings, playing nothing in particular; maybe he was only trying to console himself. A breeze had risen and was blowing away the clouds, clearing the sky. Gradually, a sliver of moon was uncovered. Some scattered stars seemed to burn with a cold steady brilliance. I began to feel better; in about twenty minutes we would be back in the harbor from which flight to the safety of the old women's house would be easy. And little by little, I fell into a half-doze, submitting to the rhythms of the boat and the notes that came from Dean's guitar.

I was awakened by harsh whispering, the sounds of lowered voices arguing. Half in shadow adjacent to one side of the cabin but visible in silhouette were Letty Monroe and Howard; she was on her knees with her arms wrapped around his legs and he was standing over her, bent slightly forward, his hand raised to deliver a blow. I closed my eyes. There was the sound of a hard slap. Dean's guitar fell to the deck with a thump. He jumped up and ran toward the Monroes.

I was going to be sick. I jumped up and hurried to the narrow ladder that led down to the W.C. My hand clapped tightly over my mouth, I managed to reach the toilet just in time. After I vomited, my face was covered with sweat, but I felt better. I leaned over the tiny sink and splashed cold water on my hands and face. As I raised my head to reach a paper towel, the door burst open and Letty Monroe virtually fell into the small cubicle. I was mopping at my face, but I lifted my head to look. She stood slumped against the door with her fist against her forehead. A purple bruise was spreading across her cheek. She closed her eyes briefly, opened her mouth and spoke quickly, in spite of her drunkenness:

"Please do what we want you to do!"

I stared at her; I really didn't understand what she meant.

With terrified eyes she sought my consent. "Please! It's the only thing I can do for him! We'll get rid of those kids and you can stay on board, or else come back after they're gone."

I shook my head. I still didn't understand.

Letty's voice rose. She choked back a sob: "Please!"

I thought I could feel the boat slowing down. I was determined to get ashore as quickly as possible.

"If you don't do it, he's going to beat me."

"Why do you stay with him?"

"What else can I do?"

As I pushed past her, Letty Monroe hissed: "You'll never get that part you want so badly!"

Without answering, I climbed back onto the deck, relieved to see that we were moving into the harbor. The ropes had been untied; we were gliding toward a mooring. With his guitar bundled against one arm and Rosalie against the other, Dean was standing close to the side. They grinned at me. Howard Monroe was standing in the same spot where he had hit Letty. His arms were folded tightly across his chest and his eyes were narrowed in an obsessive stare.

Crouching on the deck, his figure partly illuminated by the light slanting down from the moon, was Gerard. He had put on his straw hat again, and its brim shadowed half his face. He was holding a cigarette between the slender fingers of his left hand and scratching his toes with the fingers of the other. The last thing I remember seeing when I left the boat was the luminous glow of the one eye that was not obscured by the drooping brim of his hat. This eye seemed to follow me, expressing a desire that was weighed down by despair. For an instant, an instant that I recognized as perilous, I paused, meeting Gerard's mute appeal with tentative consent. In my belly was a lurching sensation. Quickly, I turned away, suppressing my longing to clasp him in my arms, and quickly, too, I stepped off the boat and onto the landing area.

I sensed a terrifying menace in this stark and unexpected passion. And when I was back in my room in the house of old women, I wept, invoking my children's memories and their names to save me from a doom I could not even begin to define.

When I finally fell asleep, I felt the chill of dank icy water closing over my head and not even the images of my children could prevent me from plunging into the depths of a nameless disaster.

The third floor of Esma's house shakes with the rhythms of lively Balkan music. A blue tunic over her pink dress, Esma turns and whirls with arms extended, turning in time to the music while she plays a counter rhythm with the round brass cymbals she wears on her fingers. In his two small hands Radovan clutches a large horn, raising it high and blowing energetically, while nearby, bouncing and bobbing in her blue velvet dress, curls flying, Rosalba beats the double-headed drum she holds tucked in the crook of her elbow. Tamara and Sasha sit on the floor, swaying to the music. With a wide red sash around his waist, Dionysios at last has begun to seem a member of this merry family. To the act of making music, I observe with satisfaction, he can abandon himself with laughing energy.

With shouts and stamping, Esma and her children explode into sound with a boisterous gypsy song called "Cigane Moj." Even I can translate this simple phrase into "Gypsy Mine." I listen, yearning to move but restraining my feet because of my ignorance of the steps. Surely someone will help me out!

But no. The musicians play. The singer sings. Esma is a one-woman band, singing, dancing and playing the zills all at once, tapping her feet, shaking her shoulders, jewelry jingling in time to the music while she sings, shouting every so often to urge the others to move faster. As Esma flies around the room, her long blue tunic flares around her body in circles.

Dionysios plays the guitar. Radovan blows the horn. Rosalba beats the drum. Esma sings and dances.

"Cigane Moj" is immediately followed by a throbbing dramatic song called "Djelem, Djelem." Esma sings it with her head thrown far back, hair swinging as she sways, her hands and arms carving space before her body. More an instrument than a woman, every feeling transformed into soaring ecstasy, Esma sings. It's a gypsy ecstasy, the ecstasy of sorrow.

Far into the night the music continues. Not even the children seem tired. And after a while I myself no longer care whether I look silly, and I drift into the dance, turning and whirling, spinning in a dreamy meditation that needs no partner.

Swaying from side to side, Rosalba beats the drum with her palm. Tapping one foot as he blows the horn, Radovan plays the melody while his mother sings a lilting song, and Dionysios, hands moving over the strings of his guitar, also begins to sing, adding his high plangent voice to Esma's.

Finally, Esma herself brings the entertainment to a halt. Stripping off her cap of gold coins, she drops to the floor like a limp flower, skirts forming a fantastic blossom around her body. She fans herself with a fluttering brown hand.

Dionysios and his mother exchange rapid words.

After a while, Esma gets up, thanks me for the painting, hugs me, and chirps "Good night." Leading Tamara by one hand and Sasha by the other, she leaves the room with a swoosh, followed by Radovan and Rosalba. Just as he is about to step outside into the hall, Radovan looks back over his shoulder and gives his grown-up brother a long wink.

With a tired smile, I follow Dionysios down the narrow stairs to the first floor, very tired, almost exhausted and yet unwilling to go home after so much pleasure. I want to go on dancing all night long, and I do *not* want to say good night to Dionysios.

As we pass the kitchen the same old women stare at me, whispering and pointing, repeating "*Amerikanka. Evo Amerikanka.*" Wondering whether Esma has a whole gypsy encampment in her kitchen, I ask Dionysios: "Who *are* all those old souls?"

"People Mother takes care of. She supports them."

"I can see that," I answer, a little amused by his pride in her.

In the moonlight, the road lies ahead like an unfurled ribbon of tinsel. The quiet of the island seems to enfold the mist-shrouded hills in deep silence, an air of watchful gentleness, a mute reminder of a wound experienced long ago yet never to be dismissed entirely by a memory stubbornly retentive of pain, recalling the sorrow again and again to a sense of loss too raw ever to be healed completely, even by the soothing hand of a lover, or by a passion too compelling, too savage to be denied.

The deep-textured silence of this night enfolds me in a languor that is deepened by the presence of the man at my side. His profile is a composition of striking clarity, a cameo of superb masculine beauty. In silence, not touching, we walk along the road that coils above the town, ascending the hill on which my small house sits high above the Adriatic Sea.

Who is this man, I ask myself, who has invited me to glimpse the harsh losses of his life while maintaining a strict reticence about mine, about which he knows nothing at all, about which he has asked nothing at all. Maybe he does not *want* to know about my life. Maybe he is afraid that personal knowledge might impose a weightier obligation or, more dangerous still, an invitation to care about me.

As I listen to the water swaying against the steep rocks that surround the island, I find myself drifting toward a mood of acceptance that somehow, as my feet carry me nearer and nearer home, relieves me of a merely conventional need to know more about the man who walks with me than the glaring outlines of his pain. I feel that he is trapped in a silence of brooding unhappiness and yet he seems to give off an aura of relaxed, if resigned, readiness for whatever might occur between us in the secretive calm of this night. It is a shock when his voice cuts into the silence with a roughly articulated apology, or is it a plea:

"I must seem very bitter."

"Maybe a little. But wouldn't almost anyone feel bitter who had some of your experiences?"

With a shrug, he criticizes himself: "I don't have a very resilient nature. Anyway, my life is a wreck right now."

A familiar resentment flushes over me. I tell myself that he is asking for sympathy. Dionysios is just another man begging for a woman's understanding support. And even though I vow, for self-preservation, to withhold what he seems to be demanding, I nevertheless hear myself respond in a consoling tone: "But now that the political part of your life is over, can't you go back to your singing career?"

"It's not really my career that's a problem. I can always pick it up where I left off. It's more that I didn't want to meet a woman like you. At least not now."

I say nothing because his reserved tone causes me to envision a still birth, to see clearly before me a new thing that has been fertilized and seeded, nurtured, born, emerging from the mother's exhausted body, an unformed mass of tissue. Dead before born, this aborted love comes too soon.

Placing his hand lightly on my arm, after an elaborate apology for even mentioning her name, Dionysios explains: "You see, Divna was about as capable of devotion as a cobra. In some ways, she was deadly for me."

"Maybe her idea of marriage was different from yours." The topic of Divna has given me a clear and almost welcome sense of security; I tell myself that Dionysios is still ensorcelled by a tortured attraction to her. To test this, I tease:

"Well, maybe you and Divna will get back together again."

He gives me a quick irritated glance. "You don't understand. Everything's over with her. I'm trying to say that, in spite of it all, there's a certain—" Breaking off in frustration, he turns away and resumes walking up the silvery road. There is suppressed anger in his movements.

When I catch up and am again walking at his side, Dionysios looks at me with a defeated air. "You're right not to trust me. You think I was just playing a masquerade with you. What woman would trust a man who'd do that?"

"No, no, it's not that," I protest, laughing. "Our adventure was intriguing. *'Cos'e tal mascherata?'* Until you came visiting in your fisherman's disguise, life here was becoming—not exactly boring—but anyway, too predictable."

"I'm sorry. You see, so many women come here looking for rugged primitive types. You can't imagine! And then, I couldn't understand why you weren't at least a little bit afraid of me." I can feel the intensity of his gaze and I interpret it as a plea for forgiveness.

"Let's forget that part of it. I suppose you *did* make a fool of me. You did humiliate me, in a way. But that's in the past."

"Do you remember the night we went swimming in the dark?"

"Of course. How could I forget *that?*"

"I wanted to be closer to you, but—"

"Well, if you did, you kept it well hidden."

"I was afraid that if I frightened you, I'd never see you again."

"'Frightened' me? *How?*"

"By being too intense."

I pull away from him with a slight sense of panic. Waves of pallid moonlight quiver above the road, vibrating in the thick darkness like long fingers strumming an instrument.

"You are very tempting, Miranda." A sudden change of mood. He pretends to leap at me, to chase me to the side of the road.

"Me? Tempting?" I play his game with an ironic sense of fun that masks both the compassion and the attraction he has aroused in me. In my backward flight, I stumble over a branch lying in the road and am caught around the waist by his quick hands, hands I cannot see in the dark but whose warmth I can feel, hands that I have invited during the secret daydreams of long sunny afternoons to rove my body, hands that have gently opened the passageways of this body to welcome a total embrace.

After his arms have closed around me, his lips seek my mouth in a long kiss that is rough and assertive, almost harsh in its long-denied ardor. Our lips open and close in small teasing bites at the same time he presses me tightly against him; it is an embrace of desperate intensity. When I had been hoping to discover delight, the pleasure of abandoned amorousness, I find a greater heat than I am prepared to withstand.

We walk deeper into the wood at the side of the road, gently moving toward a sturdy tree. I lean against the trunk, waiting while Dionysios caresses my thighs with his warm hands, gathering my skirt around my waist, repeatedly stroking the moistness between my thighs before pulling down my flimsy pants and helping me step out of them.

When he enters me with a precise and loving exactitude, this man ignites a knot of fire deep in my belly. I am startled by my own fierce exclamation of pleasure. Closing my eyes, I rest my

head against the tree, lips parted, gasping. I am quietly happy,
enjoying the flush of satisfaction that spreads through my body.
I clasp him tighter, listening without believing the love words
he murmurs against my face.

But suddenly, almost violently, Dionysios ends his love
chant. He pulls away and turns toward the road.

"What's wrong?"

He shakes his head vehemently. His tone is urgent and
frightened. "Let's go."

Smoothing down my wrinkled skirt, I follow him to the side
of the road.

"What's wrong?" I repeat, laying my hand on his arm.

Dionysios stares at me angrily, almost accusingly:

"First your paintings attracted me! That wasn't dangerous.
But now I've let myself go too far emotionally!"

Still enthralled by lingering pleasure, I am slow to experience
my own growing impatience. But gradually, my mood darkens
too. I return his anger, stating: "We don't have to see each
other again, if that's what's worrying you."

"My life's such a mess!"

"If we stop now, we won't hurt each other." Head high, I
stalk away. I stride up the hill, easily outdistancing him, because I am used to the steep slope.

Hurrying to catch up with me, he calls: "Do you mean that?
Do you? You really don't want to see me again?"

I turn and laugh sharply: "You're so neurotic! You say you've
found a woman you want. But you're afraid of me. You want to

get away from me as soon as you've found me."

"I don't know why, but I like the way you say brutal things. It's true. But then, you've never been married and failed at it. Have you?"

I shake my head. "So far I've never wanted to bury my life in another person."

"Then you've never loved anyone."

"I wouldn't say that." With a shrug I go on walking. "We have a lot to talk about."

I start running.

"Wait for me!"

I slow down, giving him a chance to catch up, but when he's close enough to touch, I shove him in the chest. "Come on, I'll make some of your foul Greek coffee."

He looks at me for a long moment. "Can we swim together afterwards?"

"The way we did before?"

"Yes, that way. Or maybe a different way." His grin prophesies mischief, and yet he seems very tired.

"Come on then! Hurry up!" I rush toward the door and when I look over my shoulder with a smile of invitation, I can see the change in his expression from distress to bemused contentment.

And I wonder whether it's too soon to show him the work I completed during the time before he came back to the island, the series of paintings that I call "Image Dance in Five Parts."

Gerard and I—it seemed—began to meet each other, at first accidentally, coincidentally, and later as if by plan; we met, secretively, furtively, adroitly, hurled together by a defiant compassion for each other, by a love we did not understand but obeyed in a mood of humble and honest servitude.

He would never capture me, I proclaimed silently, exultantly, as I hurled myself as fast as I could down the rocky slope, crashing over stacks of broken leaves. My heart was booming like a cannon under my sundress.

No, he would never imprison me. But still Gerard pursued me, slipping here and there, over the rough terrain as silently, as deftly as a barefoot savage flowing around the contours of a hill spread with green trees. Quickly, I ducked behind a thicket of bushes. He wouldn't find me there. He wouldn't be able to fling his arms around me and trap me inside his desperate harsh passion. I knew he was certain he could run me down at any moment, track me as clearly as though he were a hunting dog and I the prey, run me down, pin me to a wall and bite into me with his sharp teeth. But the sweet savor lingered, had not yet been satiated, and so I hid, crouching, in the thicket, waiting, heart battering my ribcage, one hand rubbing at a long scratch on my thigh. My dress was torn from waist to underarm. I was sweating, giving off the smell of sex.

All at once I surged out of my hiding place and streaked

across the clearing, falling back against a stone wall with both
hands pressed over my breasts. Gerard took no notice of me,
the clever hunter, but ran past without looking, bounding
across the clearing, springing to a stop at the entrance to a
cave.

Just outside the dark mouth of the cave he crouched, his hair
hanging over his forehead into his eyes, his red lips open as he
breathed heavily. One hand lifted, reminding me—ludicrously—
of the raised paw of a trained retriever, he beckoned me to
follow him into the cave. Dressed in white shorts, the neck of
his white shirt open, revealing the golden hairs on his chest,
throat arched in a sinuous curve evoking the image of a swan's
throat, Gerard beckoned to me with an insistent and desperate
claim in his pale eyes. He crouched at the entrance of the cave,
waiting for me to follow him into the darkness.

For a time I stood waiting, poised against the wall, my heart
quieted by the weight of my hands. I shook my long hair into
the wind as I waited, panting and watching as Gerard dropped
to his hands and knees and crawled inside the cave, disappearing from view. Lifting my skirts, I ran across the ground,
feeling inside my body, trembling deep in my belly, a terrifying
happiness that spurred me to run even more swiftly. My desire
was piercing.

On hands and knees planted in the warm dirt, I peered
inside the cave. Gerard was also on hands and knees, searching for something among the heaps of stones and dust. I could
not imagine what he was looking for. My groping hands slid

across patches of moss. There was a fresh smell, as after a heavy rain, and yet everything in the cave was dry and rocky. Hand resting on my throat, Gerard pulled me close. My breath was locked in my chest. I could not breathe. With a stick of charcoal in his hand, for that was what he was searching for, Gerard softly raised my chin so that my face was level with his, and he squinted, nearly closing his eyes as he bent nearer and drew on my face. His breath passed into my open mouth. Thick golden lashes nearly closed over his eyes as he drew. When he was finished making designs on my cheeks and forehead, Gerard slipped his hand into my dress and pulled it down to my waist, exposing my breasts. He carefully traced emblems on my breasts, but I could not see them in the dark.

When he was finished, Gerard cradled my naked breasts in his hands and kissed them. Moving back with a serious patient air, Gerard rested against the cave wall, knees pulled up to his chest.

Aching with desire, I crawled toward him, reaching for his penis, gently rubbing it until it swelled out of the fabric of his shorts. I opened them, softly pushing aside the material to hold my lover's penis in both hands, stroking the shaft very softly as I gradually lowered myself onto the floor of the cave, my face intersecting the triangle of Gerard's raised legs. How sweet it was to lap at the tip of this stalk, to nibble at the taut rounded flower, to suck slowly, sucking and coaxing out the fragrant liquid.

We rested for awhile, eyes closed, breath mingling.

The mood changed. Gerard abruptly dropped onto his hands and knees and began to crawl around the dirt floor of the cave in a circle. Neither smiling nor teasing, he circled my kneeling body, eyes fastened on mine, for I moved with him, slowly turning my head to duplicate the motion he traced with slow deliberate movements. Kneeling, feet tucked under, I waited, turning as he turned, not to break the embrace of interlocked gazes. We were magnetized by an unseen cord wound around our bodies by an invisible hand, a cord that was tightening with each circle as Gerard orbited my body on all fours.

Suddenly, he lunged at me. I was caught off balance and knocked backward onto the ground under him. He flung himself on me. I could neither clasp him more closely nor push him away. Hands hovering at his shoulders, I could not tell what he intended by this assault. I could have easily shaken him off. He began to shudder. Hot tears fell on my face, running over my throat and shoulders, trickling into the dirt. Sobbing, he held me until I too was moved to an inarticulate mournful and startled love, stirred to provide a response as sorrowful as his rough sobs.

We lay for a long time in each other's arms, sobbing from a shared and mysterious happiness. We had been visited by the stranger god called passion.

At last, exhausted, we shifted our weight and stared at each other in silence until gradually our desire, which grew with its fulfillment, demanded another embrace. Faces streaked with tears and dirt, bodies stained, tense, still, with ardent expectation we lay head to toe, toe to head, and buried our faces between each other's thighs to drink greedily.

Finally, we lay perfectly at ease on our bed of rumpled leaves and twigs, moss and tiny stones, our bodies pressed tightly into a warm space of earth rot and pungent humus.

Later, we left the cave, laughing, weary from love. It was nearly twilight. The island lay supine, submissive in the violet light that announced the sunset.

Hand-in-hand we walked down the rock slopes, listening to the suppertime cries of the animals. The goats were hurrying over the hills, their bells ringing merrily. Along the winding roads shepherds were driving their flocks. Occasionally, a plaintive bleat was heard. In the farmyards scattered here and there among the dark green hills, women were standing, clucking and crowing as they offered the evening corn to flocks of chickens that strutted about. In the distance a farmer called "Soooooooowie," in a high harsh voice.

It was dinner time on the island. No Angelus but this, the melodies of hungry beasts.

I could hear music coming from the other side of the wall. I listened more intently. Yes, it was music. In the house next door a woman was rocking her baby to sleep, no doubt, singing to the child in a deep amber-toned voice that made me feel as though honey were flowing into my body, softening and dissolving the tensions that so often—ever since I had begun to meet Gerard—secretly of course—made me want to lie down and weep. On the other side of the island, where the foam was thrown high against the rocks and the sea crashed and fell back, leaving flocks of bubbles to glide across the crests of the waves before they exploded softly in the gentle radiance of a summer afternoon, on the other side of the island Gerard was waiting for me. Fleet, delicate, deft and mute as a deer, Gerard waited for me to come to him. But in my belly the other man, Dionysios, had planted a child.

The house was empty this afternoon. Having tied their scarves over their white heads, the old women went to a neighboring town to examine some locally renowned weaving. We'd eaten a heavy meal, followed by peaches soaked in wine, and then I felt drowsy, heavy, and a little queasy; besides the new life that was growing inside of me, there was something less pleasant, an ardor that was irrational, violent, obsessive. Many times, I felt like vomiting to expel the love sickness from my body so it could not infect the child of the man I had loved, the man I once called "husband." I had no defenses against Gerard. Even then I could envision him among the rocks on the pale green beach where I used to splash and play alone; that afternoon he was waiting for me, lying on his side on the beach, his face shadowed by his hat, drawing circles in the sand with a pointed stick.

I stood on the balcony with a tiny cup of hot coffee in my fingers. I felt very calm, almost as though I had stepped inside of Gerard's perfect silence. Standing on the balcony with my arms on the railing, I watched the rabbits at play in the yard below. Sifting through the branches of the trees, the light splashed the grass. I was happy standing there. Up and down the narrow streets old women dressed in black were hunched on rickety chairs in front of their narrow stone houses, waiting for evening to come.

Two large brown rabbits were pinned together in a scrap of light. One was tenderly cleaning the other, hopping all about to reach every part. The rabbits put their noses together, sniffing. I smiled, feeling pleasantly warm, for Gerard was waiting for me, drawing circles in the sand. As I watched the rabbits play, a shot rang out. The larger of the two rabbits lurched forward, then dropped into a furry heap with his head between his paws. The second rabbit began to leap around the spot where they had been lying together. She bounded over to the dead animal, sniffed his flank, drew back and came closer to sniff again. While she was at the dead rabbit's side, a second shot rang out, catching her in the breast. She fell to the earth alongside the other. The coffee cup dropped from my fingers and crashed on the concrete below the balcony. Turning, my hand pressed against my ribs, I looked up at the balcony of the house next door. A long black tube had been thrust through the foliage, but I could not see the person who held the gun. Taking advantage of the old women's absence, a sly neighbor had decided to pick off a dinner or two. The rabbits would be eaten. After all, that was why they were raised, to be eaten.

Two more rabbits scurried out of the bushes and hopped into the patch of light where the others had been playing when they were shot. One of the animals jumped on top of the other and their bodies began rocking in sexual frenzy, rocking together in front of the man with the gun.

But it was time to go, I told myself, glancing at my watch. Gerard was waiting for me. I put on a white dress with billowing sleeves and a wide gathered skirt. In my hair was a red oleander blossom. I hurried, placing my basket over my arm; I was already a little late.

I seated myself atop the cliff of black rocks, my skirts spread around me, while below, Gerard was walking around, searching for unbroken shells. From time to time he looked up and smiled. Even his smile was filled with piercing dread. After a while, he scurried up the steep rocks and fell asleep in my lap.

When he awoke, I bent down, taking his chin in my hand, bringing my face to his, mouth to mouth, thrusting my tongue inside, tasting and exploring the little cave behind his white teeth. While we were kissing, Gerard reached up under my skirts and rubbed between my thighs; rubbing with excited fingers, he reached around my waist to my naked buttocks which he stroked with a slow insinuating motion. Suddenly, he raised my skirts and thrust his face between my thighs. I leaned back while he cupped the lips of my sex with one hand; raising the circle of flesh to his mouth as though he were drinking the liquid that formed steadily there, Gerard planted his mouth on the flesh that quivered and shuddered beneath his prolonged kiss.

Pulling away, laughing, teasing, I stood up, descended the rocks to the beach below. Gerard followed. When we were standing firmly on the sand, I pulled off my white dress and tossed it onto the beach. Gerard stepped out of his denim shorts, his sex fully erect. He placed his arm around my waist and drew me toward the edge of the sea where we stood flank to flank, gazing at the crests of the pale green foam that bubbled up around our bare feet. Turning my body toward his, bending over me, Gerard caressed me as he urged my body backward, a little up and forward, roughly opening me with his fingers while his hard sex, pushing up and down against my clitoris, made me produce desire's perfume.

Tumbling to the sand beneath Gerard, I held him against me while he mounted, thrusting into me. Locked in this union, which was ungraced by words, we embraced in a prolonged and breathless pleasure until the last crisis broke upon us in a series of clenched implosions that rang and reverberated like bells trapped in flesh.

Sinking, Gerard dropped down on me. His face rested against my throat. I was cleansed, then, by a cascade of tears. And though I tried to raise Gerard's face so that I could look into his eyes, this effort failed, for he was ashamed of weeping. Nonetheless, he knew that I was willing to enter into his unique possession, a lifetime of silent grief.

I tried to calm myself as I held him close. But I was frightened by the rawness of his ardor, alarmed by the ease with which I seemed to have entered like a conspirator into his domain of silence.

After my usual lunch of salted cucumbers, bread, cheese, and fruit, and a little drowsy from the wine, I often lie down, stretching out on the flat warm rocks at the edge of the sea to nap for an hour or so. This is a treat I allow myself only when the morning's work has gone well and the results come close to fulfilling my increasingly ruthless standards. Wearing only my bathing suit I lie on a towel, shielding my face with a wide-brimmed straw hat, and fall into a sleep that sometimes feels to me as final as death and surely as potent, I tell myself, embroidering a fantasy that I feel I can afford to indulge, since I know that my siesta is, after all, only a siesta.

On this afternoon I am awakened by the sound of rustic piping and the local violin, the *gusle*. Raising myself on one elbow, I rub my eyes, uncertain whether the figures who seem to be moving toward me in a procession are images from one of the multitude of dreams with which I have been visited during the past months, or whether, instead of chimeras, the group of six are not flesh and blood copies of the gypsy Esma, her two grandchildren and her two—her three—children, Radovan, Rosalba, and Dionysios. I still have difficulty regarding him as the son of his mother. The sunlight is ablaze and I experience a momentary blindness, realizing that one strap has slipped off my shoulder, exposing my breast. Hastily, I sit up, readjusting the bra of my bikini so that the children won't be embarrassed.

The ghostly figures move toward me at a slow stately pace. First is Radovan, dressed entirely in clear bright blue, the color of lapis lazuli. Every item of his clothing is ornamented with layers of silky gold fringe. As he walks, he holds his horn to his lips, gravely blowing a melancholy though ceremonious tune. He is followed by his sister Rosalba. She is dressed entirely in red from the ribbons flying from her black curls to the embroidered slippers on her feet. Her gold bangles jingle as she walks with a little sway, already imitating the seductive movements of the older gypsy women. Tucked under her chin Rosalba holds a small *gusle* on which she accompanies her brother. Sasha and Tamara follow somberly, dressed in finery as gaudy as that of their young aunt and uncle.

Usually opulent, today Esma wears black, a dense velvet costume enriched by spiraling gold embroidery. Her hair is bound in a turban edged in gold coins. In one hand she holds a tambourine from which gold and silver ribbons flow. On her arm is a large basket covered with red and gold woolen cloth, while in her other hand Esma balances a silver tray which holds an assortment of small cakes and other sweets. On Esma's usually merry mischievous face is a strangely subdued smile that arouses my curiosity because of its gravity. Sasha wears his habitual sulk, but Tamara surprises me with a faint smile. Does she know something I don't?

Bringing up the rear of this small procession is my lover. Grown wild and curly, his hair hangs to his shoulders, slightly feminizing his features. Instead of the white shirt and black pants he usually wears, today Dionysios appears splendidly garbed in a black velvet shirt with wide flowing sleeves and tight black pants worn with gaily embroidered boots that are molded with his well-shaped legs to the knee. He is carrying a large mask carved of wood; it represents a portrait of Silenos, his eyes fierce, his hair and beard a thicket of curls.

They are apparitions, surely, I tell myself, for no one speaks to me. Not one of the family smiles or gives me any greeting. Again, I rub my eyes as a defense against the bright light. I am unsure whether the participants in this pageant are my own familiar friends, or gorgeous phantoms whose presence I have induced with a psychic force strengthened by the effects of the wine. I am particularly puzzled by the inscrutable, almost sardonic expression on the face of my lover, who seems never before to have seen me. Dionysios gives me not the slightest sign of recognition. To reassure myself of the time, the place, of my own existence, I turn to admire the surface of the quiet blue sea. It has not changed. At mid-afternoon the water of the bay is still and calm; the *Burra* has come and gone already, leaving intoxicating heat to assault the rocks of the coast. I could be tempted to escape from whatever is happening, or to suppress this, the most startling of my many visions, but Esma comes forward and takes me by the hand, pressing it in a gesture that comforts me.

Leading me behind a pile of rocks from which we cannot be seen by the others, Esma directs me to take off my bathing suit. With innate confidence in her motives but still mystified, I

obey without question. As I am standing before her naked, she
opens her basket and removes a black tunic covered with
embroidered images of the moon in all its phases from light to
dark. I catch a glimpse of something moving in the bottom of
Esma's basket. It is a small snake coiled among the other
objects she has brought with her. I put on the tunic and stand
quietly while Esma belts it around my waist with silver cords.
Upon my head she places the little tiara I was given by the
shepherd on the island of Crete and which I asked Esma to
keep safe for me in her house. All the while Esma is preparing
me for whatever is to come, the children continue playing tunes
so solemn that they seem to be dirges. Violin and horn sing a
lament together while my lover stands dressed in his romantic
costume waiting beside the sea in the sunlight, an image of
black on gold.

When I am ready, I obey Esma and go to stand beside
Dionysios, allowing him to clasp my hand tightly. A gentle
breeze surprises us, appearing at the hottest and usually the
calmest time of day; it lifts my hair from my neck and sends it
streaming; it inflates Dionysios's full sleeves and blows his
black hair off his wide forehead. It flies under Esma's skirts,
flapping them around her legs.

Gazing quickly at my lover, I catch an unexpected look of
shyness. Is this the same man who brazenly disguised himself
as a fisherman, invaded my island solitude and seduced me
with an ease that shocked me? Now his love seems clouded by
reticence. He doesn't even return my smile. We stand side by

side, dressed in black, joined by clasped hands while the breeze embraces us, billowing our clothing like the flags on a steepletop. Esma gently positions Sasha and Tamara on my right side, joining Sasha's left hand to my right hand; their demeanor reflects that of their father.

The sea darkens a shade, though the sun hasn't yet started to descend and is burning steadily as ever. Esma reaches into her basket and takes out a long rounded piece of wood, an unmistakable phallus. She lights the end of this object, transforming it into a torch that flames in the sunlight. Esma then waves it around our heads while she chants. When she has consecrated us, Esma walks to the edge of the sea and hurls the blazing phallus into the water. When it hits the waves, hissing, Esma rises on her toes, whirls around two or three times, gives a merry-sounding shout, drops back to her feet, rushes to the spot where Dionysios and I are standing and roughly shoves us into each other's arms. Under her teasing scrutiny, we kiss self-consciously, awkwardly, without a hint of our former voluptuousness.

Abruptly, then, the mood changes. Radovan and Rosalba switch tunes and begin to dance around between songs, shouting and laughing. They grab Sasha and Tamara and teach them the simple steps of their dance, and as they stomp through the sand, the somber looks turn to those of gaiety. Esma opens her magic basket again, lifts out her pet snake and places him on the warm rocks where he lies snugly coiled, observing our party. From the basket Esma now takes a red tablecloth which she spreads on the rocks, inviting us to sit down with her. She places the tray of cakes in the center of the cloth, and we are urged to taste them, along with the floral brandy which Esma fishes from under her skirts. While we three sit crosslegged eating sweet cakes and candied fruit, and sipping the heady aromatic liquor, the children join hands and whirl around the rocks, singing. When we finish eating, Esma swoops up the remains of our feast in her tablecloth, walks to the edge of the sea and hurls the leftover food into the water for the dolphins and the fish.

Though it is still mid-afternoon, we all dance in the heat until our heads reel from the brandy we have drunk in innumerable toasts to one another. Dionysios's boots come unlaced. His crown of flowers falls over one eye, transforming his look of austerity to rowdiness.

As I dance, the flounced train of my dress whirls around my feet in splashes of black and silver, adding to the light of the sun burning above our heads the luminous glow of the night. We dance on and on until the sun begins to descend, gliding imperceptibly toward the horizon which it will eventually ignite with flames of garish rose.

Much later, after Esma and the children have kissed us goodbye, returning to their house in the town, and Dionysios has taken off his velvet costume and is once again the man I recognize, I become aware that on this day, with the sun as my witness, I have become the bride of a penniless gypsy singer.

Part 4

The mistress of the labyrinth always remained within the sphere of the Cretan Dionysios. She carried her child with her into the underworld. Was she a "mortal Aphrodite" who dies with her unborn child.....?

Gerard and I

Bodies suspended in a dance of polarity, facing each other, we are like poppies blowing in a field of grass. We are rumbling bees, circling, fragile but determined birds swooping around a fragrant bush drooping beneath magenta flowers. We are ivory tapers flickering in the pale dawn at head and foot of a dimly burning casket. We are the purple ribbons on a mourning wreath, filaments intertwined to make an ornament of glossy purple satin. We are the artifice on this tribute to death.

As we dance, suspended above the earth, whirling forever in each other's arms like the lovers invoked by Dante, we are either doomed or blessed with perpetual motion. We are condemned to an eternal embrace, flitting above the surface of the dancing floor as we smile into each other's frightened eyes.

Dimly, I realize the deep truth of Rimbaud's pronouncement: "*Je suis un autre.*" I've become someone else. The children haven't saved me. The mysteries have abducted me and now they are brutally devoting me to their obscure purposes.

THE TIDE IS STRONG AND THE SEA IS BLACK . . . . Hair flattened against my throat and shoulders, thighs and hips pumping under my drenched white dress, I stroke fiercely toward the open sea. He plunges after me, steadily gaining with each thrust of his arms in the water. I can imagine his sleek head rising out of the sea and disappearing once more beneath the surface with each powerful stroke that brings him nearer.

I close my eyes, abandoned, smiling with terrified resignation as I swim with mindless energy through the darkening sea. Listening, I hear the splashes as our arms plunge into the water, sounds that seem to me the echoes of those louder splashes, the music of the tides as they swing the sea from shore to shore in the vast cradle between land masses, the tides rising and falling in their immense chamber, their music a harmony that shapes itself out of a cosmic concern, heedless of the animals who fling their bodies about in the chilled black turbulence of the sea.

The old women find my body lying on the sand. In black dresses, heads covered with black scarves, the women come with their red wooden wagon drawn by the frisky mahogany mare. I can feel their hands as they gently lift me from the beach, strip off my dress and brush my drenched hair off my forehead and cheeks. They roll my naked body onto a blanket. Next, they lift me to the wagon bed on which my body is to rest during the journey.

The old women line up, forming a procession, the oldest at the head with her hand on the horse's jingling bridle. They walk slowly along the beach, crossing the island's rough roads with patient care. After an hour or so, we reach a small grove thickly shaded with trees. The mare draws the wagon inside the clearing which is encircled by evergreens and densely growing bushes. In this grove there lives an olive tree claimed by the islanders to be eight hundred years old. The old women say that this tree still bears fruit.

Tenderly, they lift me down from the wagon and lay me on the ground, unrolling my body from the blanket. Forming a circle around me, they begin to sing, raising a lament that is lodged in the cells of their hearts and that comes from their lips as naturally as the air they exhale. As they sing, the old women throw hands full of dirt over my face and body. A breeze rises and gently lifts the boughs of the pine trees, shaking loose fine needles that fall upon me, mingling with the grains of earth tossed over me by their reverent old hands.

Just as the women are preparing to lead the mare out of the grove, a rain begins to fall, a warm light rain that mixes with the occasional gusts of pine needles and the moist earth and leaf mould, giving off a pungent smell.

When they have covered me completely, the women stand for a few minutes longer, chanting. Gradually, I relinquish my sense of what is happening in this sacred grove, allowing my consciousness to drift toward another realm. As the last grains of earth, pebbles and drops of rain fall on me, I feel the child move within. The child. I feel this movement as the voices of the ancient women begin to fade:

> *Clouds grow in my hands*
> *I caress my clouds*
> *and fall asleep*
> *I sleep snug as in an egg*
> *I sleep and I wait for leaves*
> *to sprout on me.*

———————

It is twilight now and I am seated alone in the small boat, paddling across a river that is murky with shadows. It is difficult to row because the surface of the river is slick and oily, tangled with scum, water-logged lily pads and beds of thickly entwined vines, their tendrils wound about themselves. There is a smell of rotted leaves and decayed flowers. I row slowly. It is difficult to see in the dim light.

On the shore behind me is a meadow filled with wildflowers. Rust, pale orange and yellow flowers blossom along the shore, creating a glow of light. The meadow will soon burst into flames.

I must cross to the other side. I do not know who or what is waiting for me there. The only thing I am certain of as I row toward the opposite bank of the river—inside of me the child still lives.

*I*N THE SEA, THE WARM GENTLE NIGHT-TIME SEA, the lovers swim silently, swimming naked, swimming wordlessly like slippery black seals, penetrating the water with their slender, naked, slowly swimming bodies, swimming around and around each other, turning on their backs to float gazing up at the sky, at the pale stars and the icy three-quarter moon, floating side by side with hands linked on the milky surface of the sea, turning onto their stomachs with their faces under the water, paddling like seals, turning and flipping around and around each other in the gentle warm night sea, the lovers swim silently together.

The man swims under the woman's body and over her body, turning over and over, fingers rubbing her nipples, fingers sliding along her thighs, rubbing, caressing, exploring, fingers caressing skin as the two bodies glide through the water side by side. A finger moves into the hidden space between the woman's wet thighs, a finger turning and twisting in the flesh, as moisture grows into moisture, she floats on her back held in suspension by the water as the man thrusts and turns, caressing the moist space of woman. She turns slowly over onto her stomach, offering to the softly probing fingers the curve of her back, the rounded wet buttocks concealing the openings of her sea-washed body before the globes of flesh are softly parted by his caressing hand.

Hands on shoulders, his hands on her shoulders, hers on his, together they dive deeper, descending until the warm water rises and they are standing facing each other, face to face, breast to chest, belly to belly, thigh to thigh, standing on the smooth rippled sand at the bottom of the sea. As one hand presses her lips against his throat, the other strokes her inner thighs, parting them into a wide-spread triangle as she rubs her hands along the shaft of his swollen penis, hands cupped, rubbing in long strokes, rubbing ardently from base to tip, hands moving rhythmically at the same time that the man, fingers caressing her sex, rubs her clitoris slowly with the base of his palm.

The man inserts the tip of his penis into the woman's body, thrusting slightly as she moves forward in the warm water, tightening around him, tightening, contracting more tightly still as she clenches, holding the man's penis inside of her while he draws back in the warm night-time sea to plunge inside more deeply, holding their embrace for long seconds before he again draws back to thrust deeper still.

Hands on the woman's buttocks, the man raises her in the water, pronged upon the spear of flesh between his thighs, raising the woman as she bends her knees and thighs, encircling the man's waist with her raised legs. Their faces brush in the water, lips searching lips, tongues parting swollen lips and darting inside warm caves of mouths as, still locked together from their shining faces to their chests, thighs and bellies, the woman and the man united, forming one full rounded creature, the one sex indistinguishable from the other, man in woman becoming woman, woman becoming man, the couple embrace and dance up and down in the sea, riding the waves with passion, with pleasure, with amusement, with liking for each other, with laughter, with excitement, with fear, with expectation, with sorrow, and with love, they dance up and down together in the warm soft summer sea, the man and woman meeting with a passion that brings awe, for each knows, knowing together, that neither the one nor the other, the man nor the woman, woman nor man, will ever after this union be the same woman or man that he or she was, has been, before their midnight mating in the warm summer sea.

All they have been is now changed....to what they are to become....together.